Out of Time

Books in the
Perimeter One Adventures series

*The Misenberg Accelerator* (Book One)

*The SHONN Project* (Book Two)

*Out of Time* (Book Three)

*The Mines of Venus* (Book Four)

# Out
# of
# Time

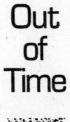

# DAVID WARD

OLIVER
NELSON

## THOMAS NELSON PUBLISHERS
Nashville • Atlanta • London • Vancouver

Published in Nashville, Tennessee, by Thomas Nelson, Inc., Publishers, and distributed in Canada by Word Communications, Ltd., Richmond, British Columbia.

The Bible version used in this publication is THE NEW KING JAMES VERSION. Copyright © 1979, 1980, 1982, Thomas Nelson, Inc., Publishers.

Library of Congress Cataloging-in-Publication Data

Ward, David, 1961–
    Out of time / David Ward.
        p.   cm. — (Perimeter One adventure series ; bk. 3)
    Summary: When Ryan Graham goes to New Denver to interview an arrogant scientist who plans a daring experiment in time travel, the Graham family and others are drawn into a race to keep the universe from being destroyed.
    ISBN 0-8407-9237-9 (pbk.)
    [1. Science fiction.   2. Space and time—Fiction.]   I. Title.
II. Series: Ward, David, 1961–       Perimeter One adventure series ; bk. 3.
PZ7.W1873Ou   1994
[Fic]—dc20                                                          94–16041
                                                                        CIP
                                                                        AC

Printed in the United States of America.

1 2 3 4 5 6 — 99 98 97 96 95 94

# Prologue

The sky was gray and cloudy on this particular spring day over the city of Denver, Colorado. Ground cars hummed busily from place to place, while thousands of people milled about the sidewalks in the downtown area.

Ten feet below Colfax Avenue, in the suburb of Lakewood, a small utility crew was in the middle of repairs. Two men wearing hard hats and tool belts were standing in six inches of water in a maintenance tunnel. The tension on their faces revealed how nervous they were, for the electrical circuit they were working on was still active. The shorter of the two men had his arms thrust inside a circuit box, trying to install a new circuit breaker. The smell of propane was strong; they had already agreed to pass the word on when they finished this job, that a gas pipe was leaking, before someone dropped a match down the hole.

The second worker held a flashlight for the first. "Watch the wrench, Lenny."

Lenny moved a little to one side. "I see it. Will you look at this, Mike? I can't believe they still haven't upgraded this part of town. It's gotta be twenty years old at least."

Lenny carefully installed a bypass circuit, safely rerouting the power, and proceeded to replace the old circuit breaker on the main line. The work progressed smoothly, but outside the clouds had opened up without warning, dropping torrential sheets of rain. Large drops of water pelted the people on the sidewalks, sending them scurrying for cover. Down in the maintenance tunnel, the water began to rise.

Mike felt the water climbing, cool and clammy, up his leg. "Lenny, the water's rising."

Lenny looked down and swore under his breath. He was ready to channel power through the main line again, but the bypass circuit was stuck. He set down the pipe wrench he was holding in the box and hastily pulled a hydraulic socket wrench off his belt. The water was over their knees when he managed to pry loose the bypass circuit a few seconds later. He jerked it out and slammed the watertight door, stowing his socket wrench on his belt.

The water rose over their waists, and Lenny started to panic. Frantically the two men waded up the tunnel to the exit, neither one giving further thought to the pipe wrench left behind, wedged between the new circuit breaker and the floor of the circuit box.

# CHAPTER 1

Millie Graham sat happily typing away at the computer terminal in her kitchen. Beside the terminal was a tall glass of mandarin tangerine juice and a half-eaten chocolate cookie. Outside, it was warm and humid, a typical late spring day in Arlington, Virginia. Unfortunately, the air conditioning unit wasn't working. The beads of sweat on Millie's forehead made her look almost feverish.

She leaned back in her chair and stretched. The house was deliciously quiet. Her husband, Dr. Nathan Graham, was hard at work at his office in Fairfax, and Ryan and Amie were still at school. Because of some accelerated courses he had taken in the fourth and fifth grade, Ryan, who was sixteen years old, would graduate from high school this year, but Amie, who was three years younger, still had four years to go. Their oldest son, Chris, was eighteen years old and finishing his third year of undergraduate work at the Space Sciences Academy on Jupiter's moon, Io.

With everyone out of the house, she was free to pursue some of her own activities, like writing reviews for a computer magazine. Millie took a sip of her drink and leaned forward to read aloud the paragraph she had just written. The "Q6ESM is designed to support molecular relays and electron caching. In a recent benchmark test. . . ." She breathed in sharply. *Test!* she thought. *Ryan has a test at ten o'clock.* She stood up and peered at the clock over the stove. 10:05. He would be starting any minute.

She prayed for him, asking God to give him wisdom and to enable him to do the best job he was capable of doing. With that pleasant little task behind her, she sat down at the terminal once more and resumed typing.

At that moment, Ryan was settling in at a desk in his advanced calculus class. The semester had gone very well up until the last couple of weeks, when he had begun to have trouble concentrating and his grades had begun to suffer. When his grades were high, his friends teased him about becoming an "egghead." They were only kidding, but it hurt just the same. On top of that, he wasn't really sure what he wanted to do about college. He had had trouble seeing a reason to go on with mathematics—until three days ago.

On one of his frequent trips to the library, he came across an article by a woman named Tatiana Rulisov exploring a rather obscure branch of mathematics. The article was fascinating, though way over his head, but what really caught his eye was her picture. She looked to be about twenty-four years old, with beautiful brown eyes, dark hair, and a face right out of a glamour magazine. He thought she could easily have been a model, even though she was already one of the most gifted mathematicians in the world.

The remarkable beauty of this young woman had struck something deep down inside Ryan, and not just because she was across-a-crowded-room-drop-dead-knockout gorgeous. Somehow for him she elevated mathematics from mere academics to art form. If someone who looked like she did could unlock the secrets of the universe with a few equations, then maybe math wasn't just for eggheads after all.

Ryan looked at his chronometer and discovered with horror that class was half over. All thoughts of pretty young researchers flew from his head as he scrambled to finish the test in the time remaining. He worked as fast as he could, but the growing panic in the pit of his stomach was slowing him down.

With only minutes to go, he knew he wasn't going to make

it. He also knew that if he had had more time he could have aced this test. When the bell sounded, he was only halfway through. The frustration and humiliation made him want to kick himself. Reluctantly, Ryan stood up and took his test to the front of the room. He handed it to the teacher, Mr. Smaully, and started for the door on the heels of the rest of the class.

"Ryan?" Mr. Smaully said evenly.

Ryan stopped and turned, looking like a trapped animal. "Yes, sir?"

"Please have a seat. I'd like a word with you."

Ryan's cheeks flushed hotly, and he sat down near the door, staring at the desk top. When the last student had left, Mr. Smaully closed the door and sat down next to Ryan.

"Your test was only half done. What's going on?" Mr. Smaully asked.

Ryan didn't look up. "I don't know. I'm just distracted."

"Well you better get undistracted, or you'll be looking at remedial work just to pass."

"Remedial work? I could have aced that test."

"I know. That's what bothers me. During one of your independent study periods, I want you to have a talk with your counselor."

Ryan would rather have done almost anything else than that, but he was in no mood to argue. "Okay. I will."

Mr. Smaully stood and opened the door in dismissal, and Ryan hurried into the hallway without looking back.

"Time's up. It's your move."

Garrett Alger leaned back in his seat, repositioning his thick glasses on his nose and eyeing the chess board with suspicion. He had sandy hair and a head that was slightly too large for his body. At twenty-nine, possessing several doctorates, he was already a legend in the world of science. "Don't rush me, you dog."

Chris Graham laughed, sounding rather more smug than he intended. "All slander to my good name aside, we agreed on a three-minute rule."

"I'm sorry your brother ever came out here."

Several months before, Chris's father and brother—Nathan and Ryan—had visited the Space Sciences Academy on Io. Nathan worked for a large communications company called SAFCOM, and had had business to attend to at the Io Converter Station, one of SAFCOM's key relay stations. Ryan had come along to check out the academy.

Chris had convinced his younger brother to play chess with an intelligent machine he and Garrett had built with the help of some friends. The trip nearly ended in disaster when the machine was stolen and went berserk. But once things quieted back down on campus, Chris and Garrett started meeting once a week to play chess. Lately theirs had become something of a grudge match, so they had chosen Garrett's private laboratory to allow them to play without interruptions.

Garrett advanced with his remaining knight in a last-ditch attempt to go on the offensive. Chris countered with his rook, taking his friend's queen and trapping his king. He grinned infuriatingly, and Garrett lurched to his feet in disgust. The look on Garrett's face was so threatening, Chris had to laugh.

"You've got an IQ higher than my weight and you still can't beat me at chess."

Without a word, Garrett walked over to one of the workbenches, grabbed a gas torch, and lit it. The mirth left Chris's face as Garrett approached the table.

"What are you doing?"

Garrett made no reply but leaned over the chess board and melted Chris's king where it stood. He turned off the flame and straightened up.

"Good strategy is not always a match for superior weapons," he said matter-of-factly.

Chris stared for a moment in incredulity at the little pile of slag on the board, even as a smile played at the corners of his lips. Garrett, he decided, was at the very least an interesting opponent.

"Of all the sore losers I've ever met, you've gotta be the worst. No . . . wait a minute. That's not true. About a year ago, I

4

almost got pushed out of an airlock for winning a game of poker."

Garrett returned his torch to the workbench and sat down again.

"I want more time. How about a five-minute rule?"

Chris nodded and turned the board around.

"Clean up your mess and find another king."


Nathan Graham sat, as he did nearly every afternoon, with one ear glued to his communicator. He had been talking to the communications manager in Denver for nearly forty-five minutes and his ear was starting to ache. Norm Grange was one of those employees who felt compelled to inform his superiors—in exhaustive detail—of every operational abnormality in his network. This meant that most people avoided talking to him.

"Norm, if it's affecting all of the systems you listed, I really doubt that it's sabotage. Tell me again what is causing the brownouts."

"As near as we can tell, some woman named Rulisov at the Technology Center ran an experiment that put a serious drain on the entire transmission grid. We asked her to notify us in the future."

Nathan set the communicator down and switched the call to his speakerphone, nursing his ear. "Right. It sounds to me like that's all there is to it. To be on the safe side, you could get some uninterruptible power supplies for your comm nodes."

"Do you really think that will be sufficient?"

"Absolutely. Let me know if the problem persists." Before Norm had a chance to say another word, Nathan terminated the connection, let out a long sigh, and put his face in his hands. He realized that as the largest communications company in the solar system they were a natural target for subversive activities, but he wished that middle management would not be so quick to attribute equipment failure to sabotage.

More than anything right now he wanted to go home, but there was another call waiting from the Denver Federal Center, which was just down the road from the Technology Center.

Maybe he could get a different angle on this power drain business. Besides, if he didn't talk to the director, the press might get wind of it and he would have a real mess on his hands.

Nathan picked up the communicator and keyed in the number for the Federal Center, gearing up for another long conversation.

Ryan hated meeting with his counselor, Mr. Brock. He was a nice enough guy, but lately he had been asking a lot of difficult questions, mostly about what Ryan wanted to do with his life. Today was no different except that he sounded wounded, as if Ryan had let him down.

"So tell me what happened," Mr. Brock said solemnly.

Ryan fidgeted, but there was no way out. "Um, I guess the test was so easy, I started daydreaming."

"What about?"

Ryan hadn't expected to have to go into detail, and he blushed before he was able to choke out an answer. "Tatiana Rulisov."

Mr. Brock smiled in spite of the seriousness of the situation. "The person or her work?"

"Her work, of course."

"Of course. When we talked last, I got the impression you wanted to pursue math and science. What's slowing you down?"

Ryan thought for a moment. "I don't know. I guess it's just hard to picture it."

"Do you see yourself as a scientist in a lab, or a professor, or a writer?"

Ryan shook his head. "That's the problem. I can't picture any of those things."

There was a long pause, and Mr. Brock frowned. "Maybe we need to adjust your picture." Ryan raised his eyebrows. "How would you like to meet Tatiana Rulisov?"

Ryan suddenly felt considerably more energetic. "Wh . . . sure! But how?"

"As you know, one of the requirements for graduation is to interview an authority in your chosen field and write a thirty-page report. I read somewhere that Tatiana Rulisov is working at the New Denver Technology Center. Why don't you fly out there and try to see her?"

Ryan shook his head incredulously. "She's gotta be way too busy."

"You never know until you try."

A giddy feeling of excitement crept over Ryan. "This is great!" He burst to his feet with a silly grin on his face and headed toward the door. "Thanks, Mr. Brock."

"Let me know what you find out."

Ryan ran out of the office, down the hall, and up the ramp to the circular commons where the lockers were. A quick call to his mom brought him back to Earth in a hurry: He would have to discuss this great idea with his father that evening. One thing for sure, it was going to be a long wait until dinner.

At that moment, Tatiana Rulisov was in her laboratory in the New Denver Technology Center, swearing at a piece of equipment. She looked as if she hadn't eaten, slept, or washed in days. Her greasy hair was slicked back with an elastic band, and her complexion was sallow and pasty. She was wearing filthy overalls under a shabby lab coat and soiled tennis shoes on her feet. As her assistant watched helplessly, she tore a circuit board out of the machine and threw it on the floor.

Tatiana's brown eyes flashed as she yelled, "You insect! I told you a hundred times the sixty-forty goes in the phase inverter. If I hadn't checked your inept work, we would have burned up the temporal logic circuit. I'd have better luck working with a clever seven-year-old."

Mione Arryoto was an attractive, dark-haired young woman of twenty-two. At the moment she was too tired to be hurt by Tatiana's insults. They had been working eighteen hours at a stretch to get this experiment working in time for a demonstration that was now only two weeks away.

Five months previously, after a string of unsuccessful trials, the director of the Technology Center had made it clear that if Tatiana's next experiment failed, her position at the Center would be given to someone else. Tatiana had chosen a challenging project, one she thought worthy of her impressive abilities. Even before the first round of testing she had brashly contacted the media and set up a date for the demonstration.

The source material for her project was a new branch of mathematics called *Subtemporal Irrelativity* discovered by Garrett Alger. He had developed it as the subject for his doctoral thesis in mathematics at the Space Sciences Academy on Io, and the doctoral committee had made his thesis generally available to the scientific community. Only a handful of scientists could understand the simpler aspects of SI, as it had been labeled, and Tatiana had decided that she was going to be the first to demonstrate a working knowledge of it.

After many long weeks of hard study she grasped the basic concepts. By altering some of the equations, she uncovered permutations that suggested the possibility of time travel. This seemed to her both exciting and flashy enough to be the subject of her project for the media, and she set about developing a suitable physical demonstration.

Once her plans were approved by the director, she hired Mione Arryoto as her assistant. Mione was a gifted researcher, but the scope of Tatiana's project was so completely new that much of their initial work was trial and error. Things had been going wrong since day one, and Tatiana had quickly gotten into the habit of blaming Mione.

Mione quietly picked up the broken circuit board that Tatiana had dashed to the floor. "I'll get a replacement from the storage room."

"Yes, why don't you do that," Tatiana said sourly, "and while you're at it, bring the capacitor back out here."

Mione was surprised by the request. Their last use of the capacitor had resulted in some nasty calls from the power company. "I thought you decided not to use it."

Tatiana gritted her teeth and spoke condescendingly, as if to a disobedient child. "I changed my mind. The utility breakers trip at one point two seven gigawatts, and I'm calibrating the system above that number. Once the breakers trip, it will still take eighteen milliseconds for the positron field to form. We need the capacitor to give the field time to stabilize."

Mione shook her head. "I think you should talk it over with the power company."

"Out of the question. If they say no, we have no demonstration and I lose my grant."

"But why do we need so much power?"

It was a reasonable question under the circumstances, but by now Tatiana was livid. She spoke in measured phrases, her voice like ice.

"I am going to push a block of lead one minute into the future. The size of the block that can be moved along the temporal dimension is limited by the amount of power available. Matter has a tremendous amount of temporal inertia. According to my calculations, we can achieve a block size of just under two inches using all the power available. This is barely large enough for a satisfactory demonstration. Remember, these are going to be slow-witted representatives of the media, not a group of brilliant scientists."

Mione bit her tongue to keep from saying anything more in protest, and walked without a word to the storage room in search of replacement circuit boards.


At the dinner table that night, the Grahams had a lot to talk about. Millie had made a wonderful meal of sour cream spinach and meatloaf. Neither Ryan nor Amie were big fans of spinach, but Millie's recipe called for a tasty mix of browned butter, flour, and sour cream with the vegetable. The dish was a favorite of the entire household.

Once the meal was over, Amie excused herself to call a friend and Ryan saw his opportunity. Tentatively he broached the subject of an interview with Tatiana Rulisov. Nathan did not take to the idea right away.

"It's a bit much, don't you think?"

"My counselor seemed to think it was a good idea."

"Your counselor?"

"Yeah. It was his suggestion."

Millie smiled kindly. "Why couldn't you just interview someone here in the area?"

Ryan flushed slightly, but his voice remained steady. "I'm interested in her work."

Nathan folded his hands on the table in front of him. "I've always done better on projects that were interesting. Since you seem to be interested in this woman and her work, I don't see any reason why you shouldn't go to Denver. So long as you don't miss too many school days."

Ryan stood up. "Thanks, Dad!"

"Wait a minute. What are you going to do first?"

"Oh. I hadn't really gotten that far."

"Why don't you write her a letter? Tell her what you have in mind, and ask her if it would be all right."

"I'll get started on it right away."

"I'm sure you will."

Ryan ran out of the kitchen and up the two flights of stairs to his room. Millie stood up to clear the table.

"Do you think it's all right sending him off alone like that?"

Nathan began to stack plates. "He's smart, and he's got good judgment. Besides, he needs a break. This math thing has really been frustrating for him."

"I suppose. I just hope we're doing the right thing letting him go."

"He'll be okay. Don't worry."


Light levels in the laboratory were dim. On the workbenches scattered around the room lay an array of projects in various stages of completion. The doctoral laboratories at the Space Sciences Academy were normally well furnished, but this one had the ugly, sparse look of a garage: totally functional and no frills. It was as the current occupant desired.

At a computer workstation on one of the workbenches, Garrett Alger sat keying in lines of code. The program he was editing had, several months earlier, furnished the intelligence and personality for the machine his team had assembled in an effort to create a living mechanism. In the end the machine had turned to uncontrollable, murderous behavior. They had traced that behavior to a single event—Garrett's beating at the hands of the two men who stole the machine—which had been imprinted on the machine's learning circuits.

Garrett was hoping to use the program as the foundation for a doctoral thesis, but he needed to be absolutely sure the flaw was not in the program. The computer screen swam and blurred before his eyes, and he stood up and stretched, looking around the room. The other projects were mostly innovative devices, inspirations he had had over breakfast or late one night, but at the moment, none of them piqued his interest.

He walked out of Folsom Hall, across the field and into the Student Union Building—or SUB, as the students called it. Figuring it was about time he waded through his electronic mailbox, Garrett found a private communication booth and punched in his personal access code, bringing up a table of contents on the screen. The first item was a note from his mom.

Garrett had been raised in the town of Garibaldi on the Oregon coast. His father had worked in a marina until Garrett was twelve. But when the economy took a dive, people cut back on recreational fishing and his father was soon out of a job. His parents fought when the money got tight, and Mr. Alger left town. Garrett went to work at a fish cannery shortly thereafter, to supplement the income from his mother's small shop on the coastal highway.

School had never been much of a challenge for Garrett, and up to that point he had done only what he had to do to get by. Working in the cannery taught him some valuable lessons about what he didn't want to do with his life, and he began to apply himself to his studies. The net result was that he received a perfect score on a high school equivalency exam at the age of twelve and started college as a junior on a full scholarship as a result of his entrance exams.

Several universities vied for his application, which provided him with the necessary leverage to see that any agreement he signed would include financial support for his mother. He graduated with a B.S. in Chemistry and a minor in Religion two years later, embarking on a series of doctoral studies over the next decade.

Because of his abnormally high intelligence, Garrett had not developed many friends over the years. In grade school, he quickly learned that he had to hide his abilities if he wanted any companionship from his peers. By the time he reached high school, he had decided he would rather go through life alone and be himself, than to live a lie among friends. To make matters worse, he became younger and younger than the people in his classes as he moved up, which made him a natural target for insults and practical jokes.

One result of this was that "all the news" in the note from his mother had only to do with an aunt and two cousins that lived in Garibaldi. She closed affectionately: The big white "G" was still mounted on the hillside over the city, and as far as she was concerned it stood for *Garrett*.

The next item in his mail was a request from a large electronics company to endorse one of their products, followed by seven different requests to come and speak at various colleges around the United States. The last item was a note that he had somehow missed last time he checked his mail. It was from a woman named Tatiana Rulisov, and the unusual name piqued his curiosity.

In the note, she explained her position at the New Denver Technology Center, then went on to describe an interest in Subtemporal Irrelativity and the intention to extrapolate and experiment with some of the concepts. The note made Garrett uneasy.

He signed off and headed across campus at a brisk pace. Entering one of the student dorms, he walked up to the third floor, stopping in front of Room 315. His knock was answered by Emmanuel Hascome, Chris Graham's roommate and best friend. Seeing Garrett, Manny's broad, tanned face lit up.

"Garrett! What brings you to the land of the living?"

"Hi, Manny," Garrett said, returning the smile. "I'm looking for Chris."

"He's at the library. We missed you at fellowship on Wednesday."

"I was busy in the lab and lost track of time."

"As usual. What were you doing?"

Garrett smiled a little sheepishly. "Tinkering."

"Well, as Chris is fond of saying," Manny put on a Brooklyn accent, "you're one uv da great t'inkers of our time."

Garrett gave Manny a withering look. "Don't quit your day job."

"Still haven't developed a sense of humor, I see," Manny said jovially.

"I have a sense of humor. It's just not stuck in first gear."

"Cold, Garrett. Very cold. Happy hunting."

"If he shows up in the next ten minutes, tell him I'm looking for him."

Garrett went back downstairs and headed across the field toward the library, thinking how odd it was to be doing so much walking. Until a few months ago, he had spent all his time in the lab, avoiding the other students as much as possible. Now he was a new believer, and this had changed his habits drastically. He found himself helping others and spending time with other Christians—they called it *fellowship*—and it seemed a day didn't go by that he didn't wind up socializing. Chris, having been instrumental in his conversion to Christianity, had inadvertently become his moral compass when he wasn't sure about the right response to a situation. Garrett sighed. Sometimes life seemed so much simpler when his only concern had been for himself.

Garrett found Chris at last in a back corner of the second floor of the library, studying behind a pile of textbooks. Chris looked up and grinned.

"Well, bless my soul, if it isn't God's gift to science."

Garrett ignored the sarcastic greeting and closed Chris's book, losing the place. Chris set his pencil down with a wry expression.

"Now that you have my full attention, what can I do for you?"

"I received a letter from a researcher at the New Denver Technology Center. She wants to expand on some of my theories."

"Congratulations."

"No, that's not the point. I'm flattered, but I'm not sure I should allow it."

"Why not?"

"I don't understand all of my theories yet, and it makes me uneasy."

Chris looked confused. "How can you not understand them? You wrote them."

"Only in a physical sense. The ideas came to me out of the blue, and I wrote them down."

"You mean, you just woke up one morning with a new branch of mathematics in your head?"

"Something like that. I don't expect you to understand without a reference point. It's like building a house *ex nihilo*—'out of nothing'—and then trying to draw up the plans by walking through it."

"You lost me."

"You're familiar with the music of Mozart? He wrote melodies and harmonies of unsurpassed beauty and complexity, seemingly by divine inspiration. He may not have been consciously aware of the theory or mechanical explanation of everything he wrote. He just wrote what was in his head and let the historians and theorists figure out the mechanics."

Chris raised his eyebrows. "You mean like prophecy?"

"Yes, although prophecy is always true and inspiration may not be. But the utterance of God is rarely fully understood by the person who utters it."

Chris picked up the thought. "So it's divine insight. 'Every perfect gift is from above,' be it prophetic, musical, or mathematical."

"Precisely."

Chris was amused. "How did we get on this subject anyway?"

"I think you asked me why I was worried about this woman expanding on my theories."

"Oh, right. Why don't you ask her for specifics? If it looks risky, you can tell her to forget it."

Garrett screwed his eyes shut. "Step Three—Inquiry for Clarification."

"What are you talking about?"

"I'm reading a book on interpersonal dynamics. I'm afraid my people skills are a little underdeveloped."

Chris smiled warmly. "Garrett, you are a unique individual."

Garrett looked out the window in mock resignation. "We all have our crosses to bear."

# CHAPTER 2

The media demonstration was a week away, and Tatiana Rulisov had finally hit the panic stage. She had given up all hope of a dry run and could only trust that the pieces she had been testing over the past several weeks would work together.

When she first came across Garrett Alger's theories, she was in the middle of evaluating the effects of graviton emissions on matter. Her experiments seemed to show that objects bombarded with gravitons might move more slowly through time. This was really just an extension of the relativistic supposition that time stopped at the center of a black hole. The slowdown was imperceptible to the naked eye, but via measurements by atomic clocks, objects were shown to drop a few picoseconds out of phase when subjected to graviton bombardment. In each case, the object snapped back into phase when the graviton emitters were shut down.

From these experiments, Tatiana developed the theory of temporal inertia: Objects that are static along the temporal dimension will tend to remain stationary; or in simpler terms, if an object is not propelled through time, the object probably will not move through time. As with most such axioms, there was an air of the obvious about this one. But it was important to physicists just the same, and the breakthrough had gained Tatiana notoriety in the scientific community.

When she read Garrett's thesis on Subtemporal Irrelativity,

most of it was over her head. But significantly she was able to grasp enough to change the direction of her research. After weeks of intense study, she concluded it was possible to travel forward through the time continuum. There appeared to be only two problems: the enormous amount of power required to move even a very small object forward in time, and the necessity of generating and concentrating antigravitons, which had never been done.

The power problem was solved by "borrowing" a power station transformer, the calibration of which caused several brown-outs in the Lakewood area. The second problem was more difficult. She found that by firing the graviton emitters through a phase inverter, she could create antigravitons, but they were very unstable and survived only a few nanoseconds before reverting to their original state. Through trial and error, she discovered that antigravitons survived considerably longer in a positron field.

The positron field, however, caused other problems. In preliminary tests, the high power graviton emitters were ready to discharge before the positron field was fully formed, so she had to find a way to store the charge for a fraction of a second before firing. Purchase of an industrial grade capacitor looked like the only solution. Knowing that the power company would never approve of her setup, she decided to inform them after the demonstration.

The last piece of the system was a temporal logic circuit that was designed to monitor all components of the system and regulate the flow of power to the emitters based on the fluctuating mass of the object under bombardment. The last week had been eaten up by efforts to enhance positron field integrity and calibrate all connections to the temporal logic circuit.

At the moment Tatiana was in her laboratory, connecting the transformer to the capacitor so she could run a low-level test of the power supply. Mione came in carrying a heavy metal case and set it on the worktable.

"Here are the power couplings. And I picked up your mail."

She dropped a stack of printouts on the table next to the

metal case. Tatiana looked up from the mess of cables in front of her, sweat dripping off her forehead.

"Read it to me."

Mione thumbed through the printouts, summarizing as she went. "Junk mail . . . junk . . . junk . . . a note from the advisory board wishing you luck . . . a note from the power company requesting specification of your future power needs."

Tatiana wiped the sweat off her forehead. "Great! You were right. I should have talked to them." It was an unusual display of humility, and it didn't last long. "Fools! Why am I always dealing with fools? Oh, well. Can't do anything about it now. It will just have to wait until after the demonstration. Go ahead."

"More junk . . . a note from some high school kid who wants to interview you."

"Tell him to forget it. No, wait a minute. This could be good PR. The media loves that kind of bleeding heart garbage. Send a note to the little brat and tell him he can come out for the demonstration."

"The last item is a letter from Garrett Alger requesting clarification of your intentions."

"Now he writes me. Let him wait."


Ryan burst into Mr. Brock's office, his fist wrapped around a printout from the communications office.

"She said yes!"

Mr. Brock's face broke into a broad grin. "That's great, but can we talk about it a little later? I have an appointment just now."

Ryan noticed for the first time the student sitting across from his counselor. "Oops! Sorry."

He backed out the door, mouthing the word *later* and ran down the hallway into the commons. Locating the nearest communication booth, he called home. The tone sounded twice before Millie picked up.

"Mom, it's Ryan. I got a note from Tatiana Rulisov's office. She said yes!"

Millie deliberately put aside her apprehension for a moment. "That's wonderful, dear! How soon?"

"They want me out there in four days for some sort of demonstration. The letter says I can interview her as soon as the media pack up and go home."

"It seems a little sudden. Will you have any trouble with your teachers?"

"I think Mr. Brock will help me over any rough spots. Will you call Dad and let him know?"

"Sure. Don't forget to tell your sister. You know how she hates being left out."

"Don't worry. I'll see you later."

Ryan terminated the connection and started walking, although with no particular destination in mind. He was going to interview Tatiana Rulisov! He tried to convince himself that he was thrilled only because she was brilliant, but deep down he knew he had a crush on her—bad. It occurred to him that the math special interest group was meeting next period.

*The guys in SIG are going to be so jealous,* he thought.

Ryan realized there was a familiar, uneasy feeling in the pit of his stomach. It happened anytime he started thinking he was cool. He stopped at a fountain, took a deep drink of water, and chided himself. *Jerk. You gotta stop thinking like this, or when you meet her you'll have a great big piece of spinach on your teeth. Or worse. . . .*

He continued his trek around the commons, slightly more subdued than when he had started. What was it Dad always said? "Clean up your room." No, besides that. "Never get so caught up in your vision that you forget to do the business at hand." Right now that sounded like good advice.

Amie went straight to a friend's house after school and didn't return home until that evening. When she came through the front door, Ryan and her parents were in the middle of a discussion in the living room. She sat down next to her mom on the couch, and the conversation stopped.

"Hi. What's up?" she asked.

"We were just talking about Ryan's trip," Millie replied.

"Trip?"

Millie looked darkly at Ryan, who smiled apologetically.

"I never ran into her, and I guess it sort of slipped my mind."

Amie was trying not to burst out laughing. "Oh! You mean *the trip*—to Denver."

Ryan knew he'd been had. "You know?"

"It's all over school, silly. Everyone knows you're going to Denver to play kissy-face with Tatiana Rulisov."

Nathan looked at his son, amused. "You should have kept your mouth shut."

"I should have kept my mouth shut." Ryan sighed with resignation.

"It doesn't matter," Nathan said, smiling. "Most of the guys are just jealous. If you come back with an 'A' paper, no one's going to give you any trouble."

"What if I don't come back with an 'A' paper?"

Nathan's smiled broadened. "I'd move to Denver and play kissy-face with Miss Rulisov."

This time Amie did burst out laughing. Millie snorted and smacked her husband on the arm. Ryan picked up a small pillow and winged it across the room, just missing his dad. Nathan held up his hands in supplication.

"Sorry, sorry, sorry. It just popped out. To make up for it, I'll pay for your trip."

"You were going to do that anyway!"

"Well, now I'm going to do it to make up for my callous behavior. Unless, of course, you'd rather pay for it yourself?"

"Oh, no. That's fine. Really. Such a nice gesture. You're a great humanitarian."

Ryan spent the next two days begging, wheedling, and cajoling his teachers for permission to miss a few days of school. Surprisingly, his math teacher was the one who gave him the most trouble. In his book there were plenty of talented mathematicians and scientists in the Washington, D.C., area and he saw no need to go all the way to Denver. In the end, a few carefully chosen words from Mr. Brock tipped the scales in Ryan's favor.

The night before his departure, Ryan had trouble sleeping. He lay awake for a full hour before dropping off to sleep, and then his dreams were fitful. He was running, missing flights, getting lost, and then through a haze, he saw Tatiana Rulisov. She was radiant in a white lab coat, with her hair swept back, wearing stylish glasses that only enhanced the enchanting beauty of her eyes. She smiled, threw a switch, and there was a terrible buzzing sound. The room burst into flames.

Ryan rolled out of bed and fell in a heap on the floor. As his head cleared and the dream disappeared like smoke on the wind, he realized he could still hear the buzzing from the dream. He looked up, trying to identify the dreadful noise. It was only his alarm clock.

After a quick shower, he dressed and threw some clothes and a toothbrush into his bag, and then ran down the stairs two at a time. His mom and dad were already at the breakfast table with their toast and juice. Amie was nowhere to be seen. They exchanged greetings, and Ryan took his place next to his father.

"Where's Amie?"

Millie spread jelly on her remaining piece of toast. "She's sleeping in this morning."

"Miss 'I-won't-leave-the-house-till-every-hair-is-perfect' is sleeping in?"

"Her class is having a dress-up day. She's going as a disadvantaged person."

Ryan snorted into his orange juice. "Trying to raise the consciousness of the entire school, no doubt."

Nathan smiled. "You can't blame a girl for trying."

They finished breakfast and moved out into the garage. There stood Nathan's ground car, a sleek powerful machine with a glossy aquamarine finish. Nathan climbed into the driver's seat as Ryan gave his mom a hug. "Thanks for letting me go. I know you're not exactly thrilled about this."

Millie touched his cheek. "You just be careful. And have a great interview."

21

Ryan climbed in the car. The automatic doors closed and sealed, and the garage door opened. With a quiet rush of air, the car floated soundlessly out of the garage and headed down the street toward the expressway.

Millie watched the car until it was out of sight, all the while feeling an inexplicable twinge of apprehension—as if she might never see her son again. She shrugged the feeling off as good, old-fashioned, motherly worry, and closed her eyes, offering a heartfelt prayer for his safety.

Nathan's car moved smoothly onto the expressway. They were out before most commuters, so it would be only a few minutes before they arrived at Washington National Airport. As the car came up to speed with the rest of the traffic, Nathan glanced sideways at Ryan's shoulder bag.

"Did you really get three days' worth of clothes in there?"

"Most of it rolls up pretty well."

Nathan grimaced. "Be sure to hang them up when you get to your hotel."

"Don't worry. Do you think I was born in a barn?"

"I've seen your room," said Nathan, as the car changed lanes.

"Well, there are those who say a clean room . . ."

". . . is the sign of a sick mind. I know. And a pig pen is a good place to grow pigs."

Ryan was silenced, but only for a moment. "Maybe I could pay Amie to clean it up for me."

"I already told her not to accept less than fifty credits for the job."

"That's pretty steep, isn't it?"

"The alternative to discipline is often very costly."

Ryan smiled at that. "You should write this stuff down."

Nathan had keyed in the airport exit. "I don't have the time."

"I could write it down for you. You could pay me, say, fifty credits a week?"

Now it was Nathan's turn to laugh. "Why don't I just pay Amie to clean your room? Or better yet, I'll clean it myself and keep the money."

"That's the best offer I've had all day," Ryan said.

They pulled into the airport and came to a stop at the passenger unloading area. "Maybe I'll just chain you in the yard and feed you with a slingshot," teased Nathan in mock exasperation.

"I liked your other plan better, Dad."

Nathan got out of the car and met his son on the sidewalk. They both prayed, asking God to bless his trip. Then Nathan handed Ryan a duplicate of his ID card. After a stern warning to use the card only for emergencies, he hugged his son and Ryan shouldered his bag, walking into the terminal. Back behind the wheel, Nathan pressed his lips together, trying to shake a vague feeling of uneasiness. He put on some soft music and scrunched down into the seat, looking forward to a leisurely drive to the office.

His morning classes over, Chris walked energetically across campus, enjoying the computer-generated sun overhead every bit as much as the real thing. Some techno-twit had programmed rain for the day before, and Chris thought the sun a definite improvement. The rain was accomplished by increasing the humidity and reducing the inside temperature of the dome, which caused water droplets to condense and fall to the ground below.

The cafeteria on the ground floor of his dorm was serving, and Chris chose a lunch of cheese sandwiches, tomato soup, and fruit. He was just tucking into his second sandwich when somebody kissed him on the cheek. He looked up into two of the most beautiful eyes he had ever seen. Leigh Quintana tossed her raven hair over one tanned shoulder and took a bite of Chris's sandwich. She had come straight from a workout and had a blue sweater tied over her sleeveless leotard and sweatpants.

Chris had met Leigh when they were freshmen and they had become fast friends, but only in the last two months had they started spending a lot of time together. They were really quite serious about each other, but neither wanted to admit it. Chris raised an eyebrow at her uninvited incursion into his sandwich.

"Help yourself."

"Don't mind if I do."

Leigh chomped off another generous hunk of his sandwich, and Chris threw what was left onto his plate, pushing it toward her.

"Can I get you something?"

"No! They're taking pictures for gymnastics on Friday. I refuse to look like a hippopotamus in a nylon stocking."

Chris groaned. "Oh, please. There's not an ounce of fat on you."

"Pictures always make you look fatter than you are."

"Vanity, thy name is woman," Chris muttered.

"What was that?"

"I said . . . um . . . can it be you know what you're doing?"

Leigh was not fooled one bit. "Uh huh. You better watch it, mister, or I'll tell your mom you were rude to me."

"You leave my mom out of this. . . ."

Their conversation was cut short by a new arrival.

"Garrett! What brings you to our humble abode?"

Garrett put his tray down and joined them unceremoniously. "I did some research on that Rulisov woman. She's a capable scientist, but I think she lacks the necessary depth in mathematics."

"So? Tell her to take a hike."

"She hasn't written me back yet."

"Why don't you call her?"

"I don't know. Maybe it doesn't matter."

"Garrett, have you ever asked God for wisdom?"

"Why do you ask?"

"You've been a Christian for about three months. It seems to me you might find yourself with fewer moral dilemmas if you sought divine guidance prior to the application of your knowledge."

Leigh cut in. "Chris, you're talking like a textbook again."

"Sorry. He brings it out in me."

Garrett was still thinking. "All I have to do is ask? Cool."

Leigh snickered. "Looks like Chris is rubbing off on you, too."

"That's a terrible thing to say," Garrett deadpanned.

Chris pelted him with a grape. Garrett picked up his bowl of pudding and sat ready to launch it in Chris's direction. Then he thought better of it and set the bowl down.

"See?" Chris said. "Self-control is the beginning of wisdom. You're getting wiser already."

"I still think the universe would be better served by a bowl of pudding in your lap."

"Discretion is the better part of valor, my friend. You must temper justice with mercy."

"And you are set adrift on a sea of platitudes without a paddle. Now *fermez la bouche* before I change my mind."

As Garrett took his spoon and started on the pudding, he couldn't help thinking that men of valor probably weren't much fun at parties.

Ryan's plane was twenty minutes late arriving in Denver because of an air traffic jam at the Stapleton airport, but that suited him fine. He was finishing a nice conversation with the woman in the seat next to him. She was married, ran a small business, and still had the time to raise two children, one of whom was about Ryan's age. She had just been telling him about a fabulous water park north of Denver called *Typhoon Lagoon*. It sounded like a great place to spend a few afternoons.

The landing was smooth, and in just a few minutes they were parked at their gate. Ryan sauntered off the plane after everyone else, wandering to the main terminal and downstairs to the ground transportation area. He climbed into the first available cab and told the driver he was booked at the Rianna Hotel across from the New Denver Technology Center.

"You in a hurry?" the cabby asked.

Ryan shrugged. "Why not?"

Soon they were whisking westward on Interstate 70 at 85 miles per hour, but the speed limit was 80, so they weren't drawing any attention to themselves. The cabby was the silent type, and Ryan didn't feel much like talking, so he just sat and watched the scenery go by. After a few miles, they headed South on I-25, exited at Sixth Avenue which took them west again toward the front range of the Rocky Mountains. Ryan was amazed by the view.

Just west of town, the Rocky Mountains thrust upward from the plains, shouting mute testimony to the artistry of God. Ryan's heart soared with praise as they approached the mountains, and he had the urge to sing a worship song. A brief glance at the surly countenance of the driver made him think better of it.

They left Sixth Avenue at Kipling, and soon they pulled into the driveway of the Rianna. Ryan had seen quite a few hotels travelling with his family, and this had everything he liked in a hotel. The rooms were built around a lush, central atrium with ponds, waterfalls, and an assortment of greenery. The second floor sported conference rooms, a game room, and a fitness center overlooking a modest indoor swimming pool.

Each guest suite had a living room and a bedroom, both fully furnished. The hotel had been built shortly after the establishment of the Technology Center to handle the endless stream of scientists, dignitaries, and tourists.

Ryan's room was on the fifth floor, overlooking a beautiful expanse of green fields with ponds and a playground. He unpacked his bag, hung up two shirts and a pair of pants, and put his few remaining clothes in the top drawer of the dresser. On top of the dresser was a laminated card offering X-rated movies for a nominal fee. He picked up the card by the edge as if it were a dead rat, dropped it face down in the bottom drawer, and kicked the drawer shut.

Picking up his bag, he dumped his notebook out on the bed, and then went into the bathroom to deposit his toothbrush. He peered inside the bag to make sure it was empty, threw it in the bottom of the closet, and flopped on the bed to call home.

Millie answered on the first ring. He could tell she was trying hard to keep the relief out of her voice. Ever the dutiful son, he assured her he was all right and asked her to pass the news on to his father. After they exchanged farewells, he terminated the connection and punched in the number for the Technology Center.

"Mione Arryoto, please." It was she who had communicated Tatiana's invitation.

"We're sorry," a recording intoned, "but Mione Arryoto is currently unavailable. Would you like to leave a message?"

"No, thanks."

Ryan decided he could use a short walk, so he grabbed his notebook and headed for the Technology Center.

The New Denver Technology Center was a beautiful glass and metal structure, more closely resembling a modern sculpture than a high-tech office building. Created to promote technical and scientific research, the Technology Center had been designed as a series of specialized labs, to be assigned to professionals from all over the world.

A sign just inside the front doors offered tours every fifteen minutes, so Ryan stepped up to the guard station and put his name on the waiting list. A half hour later his name was called, and he joined a group of eight. The tour guide was an officious-looking young woman with short dark hair and glasses. She addressed the group with polished precision.

"Because of the highly classified nature of much of the research that goes on at the New Denver Technology Center, we will not be able to enter many of the labs. But I think you will find it fascinating all the same."

The group walked down the hallway, passed three doors, and stopped at the fourth. The tour guide knocked politely and was greeted shortly by a dark-skinned fellow, with large brown eyes.

"Group, this is Lantru Kurdisan from India. Lantru, would you mind showing the group what you are working on?"

"Not at all."

He led them into his lab, which was actually quite tidy, and they gathered around his worktable. He explained that he was working on a helmet with a cybernetic interface for ground vehicles. The goal was to create a way for a vehicle to be controlled by the driver's thoughts, but he was having difficulty separating emotions from directive thought patterns in the driver. Sudden bursts of emotions or strong memories could cause unpredictable and sometimes disastrous behavior in his test vehicles.

Ryan was only half-listening. He was thinking about interviewing Mione Arryoto to begin his research on Tatiana Rulisov. The tour took the better part of two hours, and as near as Ryan could tell, they never came near Tatiana's lab.

He walked back to the hotel, disappointed but resolute, and found a message waiting for him when he reached his room. Mione had called, asking him to meet her in the hotel restaurant for lunch at noon. The clock on the night table read 12:45. Ryan snatched his notebook off the bed and dashed out the door.

A minute later, breathless and frantic, he burst into the restaurant adjacent to the hotel lobby, scanning the room intently for someone in a lab coat. "Lord, please!" he said instinctively, under his breath, and he saw a flash of white on the other side of the room. He walked quickly over to the table.

"Are you Mione Arryoto?"

Mione's beautiful oriental face lit up. "Yes. You must be Ryan Graham."

Ryan nodded. "Sorry I'm late. I only just got your message."

"That's all right. Please sit down."

Ryan took the chair across from her and was trying to figure out where to begin, when the waitress appeared. Mione had already finished her meal. He ordered fish and chips and then suddenly he was alone, face to face with a stranger and at a total loss for words. After several unbearable seconds of silence, Mione took pity on him.

"I only have fifteen minutes before I'm due back at the lab. Why don't you give me an idea of why you're here?"

"Well, I wanted to interview Tatiana for my senior college and career paper."

Mione interrupted. "First, let me warn you: Never call her *Tatiana* unless you want to have your head bitten off. The safest thing to call her—to her face—is *Miss Rulisov.*"

Ryan was taken aback, but he nodded. "Anyway, I wanted to

talk to you to get a little background and find out more about tomorrow's demonstration."

"Background on Miss Rulisov? Well, she was born twenty-eight years ago in Euro-Russia." Mione's face hardened a little. "She is beautiful and gifted, and no one knows that better than she does. She graduated from Princeton in Mathematics at the age of nineteen and finished MIT with a master's degree in Mechanical Engineering two years later. She's been doing research work ever since."

"What is she working on now?"

"She thinks she has found a way to push objects forward in time."

Ryan's eyes widened in astonishment. "Pretty impressive."

"Yes. If it works."

Mione took a sip of her coffee, now stone cold. Ryan looked up from his scribbled notes, surprised.

"Is there a problem?"

"We have tested each of the components individually but not all of them together."

"Why demonstrate something you haven't tested?"

Mione leaned back in her seat. "She spent a lot of time doing research with nothing to show for it. The center said they would cancel her grant if she didn't produce something by mid-year, so she set a date for the demonstration and invited the media. She never expected to have so many problems."

"What kinds of problems?"

"Power supply, temporal logic, phase inversion—you name it. All I can say is, this better work or she's in serious trouble."

"Why?"

"Because when she throws that switch tomorrow morning, she's going to black out this part of the city."

The waitress arrived with Ryan's lunch, and Mione stood up.

"Actually, you probably shouldn't put any of that in your paper. Are you on the EDNET?"

"We have an account at school."

"Just type TECH BIO at the prompt. When it asks you for a name, type RULISOV. That should give you a nice, sanitized bio

29

for your paper. Other than that, watch the news after tomorrow's demonstration."

Mione left without saying good-bye and hurried out of the restaurant. Ryan was beginning to think he should have stayed home.

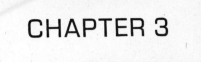

# CHAPTER 3

Back at school in Arlington, the rumors about Ryan and Tatiana Rulisov were beginning to die down in his absence. Friends and acquaintances were discovering once again that the satisfaction provided by spreading rumors is hollow at best.

For her part, Amie was trying to keep quiet about it, but there was some small part of her that would have enjoyed watching her brother squirm. In her spirit, she knew Jesus would not be pleased with that small part and made every effort not to listen to the temptation.

The bell rang, signaling the end of her English class, and she gathered up her books and headed out into the commons toward the History Center. Suddenly a stabbing pain shot through her skull, and her legs gave way beneath her. She collapsed in a heap on the carpet, quickly surrounded by concerned students.

A faculty member hurried over, cleared a path through the growing crowd, and carried her to the Health Center. Amie was conscious but woozy as they laid her in one of the beds and called her mom.

Millie was on the road seconds later, driving as fast as she dared, praying all the way. When she reached the school, she ran inside to the Health Center and found Amie sitting up in bed sipping a glass of water. Millie tried to keep her voice steady.

"What happened?"

The attending nurse left her desk and came over as soon as she saw Millie. "As near as we can tell, she fainted. We did a brain scan, but it came up normal across the board."

Millie put her hand on Amie's shoulder. "Can you tell me what happened?"

"I'm not sure," Amie replied with a puzzled expression. "I felt this horrible pain in my head and then my knees went out."

"How do you feel now?"

"I feel fine . . . like it never happened."

"Do you remember anything else?"

Amie nodded. "There was something else. Just before the pain . . ."

Millie waited patiently for her daughter to sort out her thoughts.

"There was a picture. It was like something we talked about in science class a couple of weeks ago. A long time ago, when movies were on reels, sometimes they would cut out one frame from the film and replace it with a picture of a cold drink. The eye didn't catch it, but the mind did, making people think they were thirsty. They called it sub . . . sub . . ."

"Subliminal advertising?" Millie asked.

"Right! That's what it was like. This picture just flashed in front of me."

"What was in the picture?"

"A street . . . no . . . a curb."

"That's all?"

"Yup. I think so."

Millie smiled and stroked her daughter's head. "Well, thank God you're all right. Do you feel well enough to go back to class?"

"Sure."

"Okay. But if you feel anything out of the ordinary, you tell the nurse and we'll take you to the doctor."

Amie nodded and stood up carefully. Millie gave the nurse a solemn look. "Please keep me informed."

The nurse smiled kindly. "Of course."

The scene was idyllic. Fawns leapt gracefully through a lush, green meadow as birds of myriad colors warbled in the trees. At the edge of the clearing Ryan lay under a blossoming apple tree, his head in Miss Rulisov's lap. She wore her dark hair swept back and was dressed in her lab coat.

Ryan stared into her eyes entranced. She looked down lovingly, stroking his hair and murmuring softly. The words slowly began to make sense, and he realized she was making obscure mathematical references. He also noticed for the first time that her hands were on fire, but the flames didn't burn his hair when she touched it.

A horrific ringing broke in upon his consciousness, and he was back in the stark reality of his hotel room. It took him a moment to put his hand on the communicator. A very businesslike voice informed him this was his morning wake-up call.

He put the communicator down, flopped back on his pillow, and closed his eyes. Vague images from his bizarre dreams began playing inside his head and he opened his eyes and groaned. Never again would he eat an entire large pepperoni pizza after midnight.

Light was already streaming through the window as he made his way to the bathroom. The demonstration was scheduled for nine, which gave him about forty minutes to get dressed and have breakfast.

At ten minutes to nine he walked across the street to the Technology Center. The lobby was packed with people, several of them carrying television cameras. The temperature in the room was rising, and the air already smelled of perspiration.

Nine o'clock came and went, and people began to get restless. At 9:15, Mione Arryoto appeared at the front of the crowd and asked everyone for their attention.

"It is my unpleasant duty to inform you that, because of technical difficulties, we will not be able to start until eight o'clock this evening." There was a roar of disappointment from the crowd, but she continued steadily. "Please return at that time, and I assure you it will be worth the wait."

A reporter near Ryan muttered, "It better be." People milled around, packing up cords and cameras and complaining. Ryan sauntered back to the hotel, wondering what to do for the rest of the day. Finally he decided to ask the hotel information desk for suggestions. The clerk directed him to a display full of brochures nearby.

He scanned the titles, finding mostly malls, museums, and ski resorts. He had been skiing before, but Dad had always made the arrangements and just now that sounded like too much work. Suddenly his eyes lit up.

"Typhoon Lagoon: A Wonderful Waterland of Excitement." Ryan grabbed the brochure and walked over to the bell captain's station. "Could you call me a cab?"

The bell captain glanced around to be sure no one was listening, and flashed Ryan a cheesy grin. "Okay, you're a cab."

Ryan grimaced and retorted something he had heard his brother say on more than one occasion. "Ah. A comedian. Don't quit your day job."

The man's smiled broadened. "Ground or air?"

"Air." Ryan knew the air cabs were more expensive, but he didn't want to spend any more time in traffic than was necessary.

"It will be about ten minutes."

Ryan sat down near the door to wait. A short time later, his cab pulled up and he zipped out the door, letting himself into the back before the driver had a chance to come around and open the door for him. The driver shrugged and got back behind the steering wheel.

The air cabs looked just like ground cabs, except they were sleeker and had retractable wings. The vertical and horizontal jets were more powerful, but on the ground it was hard to tell them apart.

Ryan gave the driver his father's monetary ID number and told him his destination. The driver picked up his communicator.

"This is DVSP 411 requesting an FP to Area Six, Typhoon Lagoon."

The speaker on the dashboard came to life. "Four-one-one, this is control. Your flight plan is two-one-niner. Repeat. Flight plan is two-one-niner."

"Entered and locked in. Four-one-one off out."

The cab rolled down the driveway, lifting off as it went. When they were about fifty feet up, the driver punched in the lateral jets, and they shot up in a wide arc headed north by northwest. From their cruising altitude of 200 feet, the panoramic view of the front range was breathtaking.

They sailed over the communities of Lakewood and Arvada, finally coming in for a landing on the far side of North Glenn. As they swooped down on approach, Ryan caught a brief aerial view of the water park. The impression was very much like a tropical island dropped in the middle of a suburban community, with two volcanos towering over a huge central lagoon. He glimpsed trees, pools, and waterfalls, and then they dropped below the tops of the trees.

They touched down on one of twelve landing strips and taxied to one of the numerous gates that served as entrances to the water park. Ryan could hardly stand the anticipation. He thanked the driver for the ride and hurried through the gate, courtesy once again of his father's ID.

Inside the park he was directed to the men's locker room, where he was given a wet suit, headpiece, and face mask. The face mask was equipped with a rebreather so he wouldn't have to come up for air. He undressed, stowed his clothes in a locker, and put on his gear. With the mask in place, he exhaled and inhaled cautiously. The rebreather was satisfactory. He closed the locker and had his thumb print scanned for identification, then walked as fast as he could to the far end of the locker room.

The wooden deck outside the back door looked out over a small clearing, with marked paths heading off through the artificial jungle in several directions. Three people were standing on the deck when Ryan walked out, waiting for the obligatory five-minute orientation. An attendant soon appeared, and after telling them they were here at their own risk and not to do anything stupid, he sent them on their way.

Ryan chose the path to the main lagoon. After a short walk, he emerged from the dense underbrush to an astonishing vista. Several hundred feet across, and five feet at its deepest, the main lagoon was a floor of white sand beneath a blanket of clear blue water. The two volcanos stood one hundred fifty feet high, side by side on the right edge of the lagoon, and people seemed to be everywhere, sliding down water slides, swimming in pools, falling down waterfalls.

To his left stood a board showing how long the wait was for each attraction. He walked over and found a dispenser containing maps with descriptions of the water park's highlights and safety features. Every surface in the park was lined with a waterproof, spongy material to prevent injury. In twelve years of operation, there had been only one mishap, caused by inappropriate behavior on the part of a guest.

The park was divided into five zones, with Zone One being the main lagoon. In front of the cliffs that flanked the volcanos, the water was deep enough for diving. Several water slides ran straight down the sides of the volcanos; swimmers periodically skipped across the surface of the lagoon at almost fifty miles per hour.

The left volcano was called *Gangplank Falls* and featured a steep ride up the side of the mountain in a mining car to the large pool at the top. The only way into the pool, other than jumping off the side, was by walking out onto one of the forty or so gangplanks positioned around the edge. At random intervals, the planks tilted down, dropping whoever happened to be standing on them fifteen feet into the pool.

Once in the water, the only way out was a brief swim to one of the many rounded holes through which the water drained constantly. A fall of ten to twenty feet ended in one of the many pools that surrounded the top of the volcano. A series of waterfalls connected pool to pool down the mountainside, eventually flowing into the main lagoon.

The right volcano was called *Journey from the Center of the Earth*. A short waterslide from ground level led into the bowels of the volcano. Once a set number of guests were in the dark pool inside, the water rushed upward and spilled the people out into a large trough that surrounded the lip of the volcano. Exiting the trough was accomplished via any of a number of waterslides that wound around and through the mountainside.

At *Torpedo Bay*, in Zone Two, guests were assigned their own one-person submarines and turned loose to engage others in underwater combat. The subs were equipped with concussion torpedoes, which did nothing more than give your target a good shaking.

*Tsunami Surprise* was similar to other wave pools, with a sandy beach at one end and fairly steady swells in the three-to-seven-foot range. The added attraction was the periodic arrival of a thirty-foot wave.

The last attraction mentioned in the brochure was called *In the Belly of the Beast*. The brochure starkly warned, "Do battle with a prehistoric sea monster! It will take all of your skill to subdue this hideous creature. But try not to get eaten!"

Ryan folded up the brochure and zipped it into a pocket on his chest. There was no question in his mind. He was going to have to try every attraction at least once, starting with the sea monster.

He walked to his right around the edge of the lagoon, until he came to the path with an ominous, hand-painted wooden sign indicating *Belly of the Beast*. Leaving the main lagoon behind, he headed into the jungle.

Suddenly he was subjected to a blood-curdling roar from up ahead. Not wanting to miss anything, he broke into a run. The jungle gave way to the white, sandy beach of a small lagoon. In the center of the water towered a monster straight out of every sailor's worst nightmare.

The beast stood forty feet tall, with mottled green and brown scales over its entire body. It had spines and gills and a mouth big enough to swallow a horse. At the moment, the creature was surrounded by twenty guests of the park, brandishing an assortment of lances, spears, and laser rifles. The laser rifles actually fired a low intensity beam of light. When it made contact with the monster's skin, sparks erupted and the monster howled. The effect was every bit as good as the real thing.

Another group of people stood on shore, waiting their turn. Ryan took a place in line and watched in fascination as the warriors in the water appeared to battle for their lives. One of the attackers moved in close with his lance, and the beast scooped him up, tilted its head back, and dropped him screaming down its throat. The scene was quite believable, and Ryan looked away from the gruesome sight.

As he watched over the next several minutes, five or six others met the same fate, until one of the attackers, under the cover of a furious burst of laser fire, charged and drove his lance into the beast's midsection. It threw back its head with a howl, and the belly split open, sending several thousand gallons of water and a dozen people sprawling into the shallow water of the lagoon.

The creature "expired" in a tempestuous froth of foam and sank beneath the surface of the water. The attackers who had just been freed from their gastronomical captivity shouted a muffled cheer through their masks, and hoisted the conquering lancer up on their shoulders, carrying him to the shore.

At a signal from the attendant, Ryan's group waded out into the water, greedily grabbing weapons left behind by the previous group. By the time Ryan reached the scene, there were only a couple of spears and a lance left. He took hold of the lance and stood ready, warily watching the surface of the water.

All was quiet, except for the sound of tiny waves lapping the shore. As the water began to settle, Ryan could see that the sandy bottom where the creature had stood appeared to be undisturbed, and littered with gold coins. A fellow next to him, clearly a veteran park goer, waded brashly into the outskirts of the scattered treasure.

Barely ten feet in front of him, the surface of the lagoon erupted in a cataclysmic blast of spray and sand. The beast came roaring up from the lagoon floor, reaching its full height in a matter of seconds.

A barrage of laser fire shot past Ryan's head, and he realized he was standing too close. Several spears sailed overhead, and one fell short, hitting him in the shoulder. Though the spearhead looked like metal, it was actually made of the same spongy material that lined the pools and slides. Between the protection of his suit and the softness of the spear, he doubted he would even have a bruise.

Ryan started backing away, but the monster noticed he was within reach, and its arm swooped down to scoop him up. At the last moment, Ryan dodged to one side and drove his lance into the fleshy part of the creature's hand. The impact knocked him head over heels, but he received a throaty roar from the beast for his efforts.

The hand came down again, this time grabbing the adventurous fellow who had trodden on the coins in the first place. Ryan watched with a strange sense of giddy horror as the unfortunate fellow was dropped into the creature's slavering jaws. A group of five, armed with spears and lances, charged the creature's midsection but they were easily swept aside. Two of them were caught and swallowed in the process.

Ryan picked up an abandoned laser rifle and started firing, cutting a diagonal pattern of sparks up the creature's chest. Two others stepped forward, joining their fire with his, and they advanced in a line. They concentrated their fire on the mottled belly, causing the beast to howl, and for a moment Ryan thought they were winning. Then the hand swooped down again.

He tried to dodge, but this time he bumped into the fellow next to him. The hand closed around his torso and up he went. He thrashed and screamed like an extra in a B movie, partly because it was expected and partly because the jagged teeth—which for the moment seemed to be his only destiny—looked very sharp.

He hung forty feet in the air, staring down the monster's enormous gullet. The mouth opened a little wider, the hand opened up, and he dropped head first into the darkness, landing with a tremendous splash inside the belly of the beast. When he came up, his eyes took a moment to adjust to the dim red glow of his surroundings. He realized there was an attendant on a covered platform beside the pool in which he was floating.

"Move to the side quickly, please," the attendant said with some urgency.

Ryan swam over to the side and pulled himself up so that he was sitting on the narrow ledge around the edge of the pool. No sooner was he up and out of the way, than another body came plummeting through the hole into the dark pool. This pattern was repeated several more times before there was a sudden rush of water. A wall opened up, washing everyone except the attendant out into the lagoon.

Ryan joined the group of former captives hailing the marksman who was responsible for the beast's most recent demise. They carried him on their shoulders to the shore, and the group broke up, each going his own way. Ryan took his mask off and stood for a minute to catch his breath, elated about his adventure but also relieved to be on dry ground again.

He spent the rest of the morning and most of the afternoon sampling the attractions, finally deciding he liked *Gangplank Falls* the best. There was something about being washed down the mountainside from pool to pool that he found very relaxing.

When it finally occurred to him to check the time, his heart skipped a beat. The clock read six-thirty, and the demonstration was scheduled for eight o'clock sharp. He took the shortest path back to the locker room, which meant a high speed slide down the mountainside and an arduous wade through the main lagoon.

Ryan was out the gate twenty minutes later, but unfortunately many of the other guests were leaving at the same time. He climbed into an air cab over an hour later, so it was with some agitation that he asked the driver for his best speed to the Technology Center.

He ran through the glass double doors at 8:25, feeling slightly sick to his stomach. The guard behind the front desk raised his eyebrows.

"Can I help you?"

"I'm afraid I'm terribly late for the Rulisov demonstration."

"First hallway on your left, last door on the right. Laboratory Eighteen."

"Thanks."

Ryan rounded the corner and broke into a dead run, stopping a few feet short of the door so as not to disturb the demonstration. He opened the door and slipped inside, closing it quietly behind him. A crowd of media people were packed in the lab, making it difficult to see. He moved to the left side of the room for a better view.

Time seemed to stand still for a moment. She was just as he had imagined her in his dream. Tatiana Rulisov was wearing glasses and a lab coat with her hair swept back, standing in front of a bank of machinery and addressing the group. Before her stood a peculiar-looking ray gun pointed at a small block of lead. The lead was mounted in the center of an odd-looking device with a series of prongs pointing upward from its base. Miss Rulisov spent another minute or two, finishing up her description of the machine.

". . . so the temporal logic circuit controls the antigraviton flow and particle dispersion throughout the positron matrix. Now, if there are no further questions, I will proceed with the demonstration."

Instinctively, Ryan knew something terrible was about to happen. As Miss Rulisov reached for the switch, he wanted desperately to call out, to stop her somehow. But that would be silly. The switch came down.

A hazy, bluish field formed around the block of lead, proof that the antigraviton emitter was being charged. A fraction of a second later, a mile away and thirty feet below Colfax Avenue, the circuit breaker on the main power feed to the Technology Center tripped. A pipe wrench accidentally wedged between the breaker and the bottom of the breaker box prevented the circuit from opening, and power kept coursing through the line.

In the lab, the emitter let out a high-pitched whine, and the charged field turned from blue to milky white. The capacitor

41

glowed a dull red, and before anyone could scream, there was a deafening sound like water being sucked down a pipe. The capacitor exploded.

The force of the explosion sent a massive backlash down the power line, melting the cable as it passed. When it hit the breaker a moment later, it found an exit into the tunnel. The propane in the tunnel ignited, and breaker box, tunnel, and fifty feet of Colfax Avenue went up in a pyrotechnic blast, destroying ground cars on the street above and blacking out the city of Lakewood.

Downtown in the control center for the power company, alarms went off everywhere and on-duty personnel scrambled for their stations. The chief engineer for the shift called out status from the monitoring console.

"Looks like we've had an explosion at the Technology Center. Backlash meltdown on the main power feed. Massive electromagnetic transient at Breaker ten-seven-seven."

He pulled up a grid map of the city, with the locations of both explosions lit up in red. After a brief assessment, he thumbed the communicator.

"Emergency Services! Code Yellow to J-four-two, Code Red to L-thirty-seven! Emergency Services, Code Yellow to J-four-two! Code Red to L-thirty-seven!"

On Kipling Street, in front of the Technology Center, drivers stopped their cars to stare at the strange sight adorning the night sky. At first glance, the building appeared to have been impaled by a gigantic pillar of steel, which stretched out of sight into the stars above. On closer inspection, the pillar appeared more fluid, like a column of mercury. It shimmered with a dull, amorphous light that was so alien, some of the bystanders were terrified. Traffic became a shambles as some tried to speed away, causing collisions and bottlenecking the cars packed like sardines on the road.

Surprisingly, the building was still intact, as if no explosion had occurred. Emergency vehicles converged on the scene, and police squads ringed off an area measuring a half-mile radius around the shimmering phenomenon. The scene took on an atmosphere of the bizarre. The emergency response teams did their best to herd cars out of the area and take care of the injured, but there was no fire to fight, no rubble to search for survivors, none of the crisis situations they had been trained to confront.

City officials met within the hour and requested assistance from the National Guard to help control the looting that had begun in some of the eastern parts of Lakewood. As the initial confusion subsided, the city commissioner declared a general state of emergency and notified Washington, D.C.

At the edge of the solar system, inside Perimeter Command Station, last outpost for the Interplanetary Police Force—or IPF as they were called—head mechanic Jerry Wysoski was up to his elbows inside the engine of one of the IPF Fighters it was his pleasure to work on every day.

The station was really a floating military base, created to keep the peace in the outer reaches of the solar system and to provide assistance to ships in distress. There were about one hundred men on the station at any given time, not counting those on leave or patrols. The accommodations were spare but comfortable, and they kept quite busy despite their isolated location.

The launch bay held a dozen fighters ready for launch at a moment's notice, thanks to the vigilant skill and oversight of the head mechanic. At almost any hour of the day, Jerry could be found in the launch bay, covered with grime and happily repairing one of the expensive ships.

He was tall and athletically built, with sandy brown hair and an easy smile. His first assignment had been with the IPF, but he had washed out after a friend died during a training exercise. The next ten years he spent as a freighter pilot, trying to forget, shuffling cargo from planet to planet. He would have still been at it, too, except for an episode that happened over a year ago. Thanks to some fancy flying and divine intervention, he had almost singlehandedly saved a barge full of people from certain destruction.

His heroism caught the attention of Perimeter Command, and they offered him a commission as a low-ranking officer. He accepted on the condition that he be assigned to work on the engines, not to fly. Perimeter Command agreed, secretly figuring he wouldn't stay in the launch bay for long. They were right. Within a month, he was out on sorties with the other pilots, proving to himself that he still loved to fly. The commander offered to put him on the duty roster, but Jerry decided to keep his job as mechanic so as not to be locked in the pilot's seat.

He glanced over at the LX44, an experimental craft built for high speed and one he had been wanting to take out for some time. He eyed the sleek ship much as a cowboy looks at a bucking bronco he knows he can tame. For this one, all he would have to do is climb into the pilot's seat.

Jerry sighed and turned his attention back to the business at hand. At the moment, he wished he were in the pilot's seat. For two hours he had been trying to chase down a pesky electrical problem. He had his probe isolated on the offending connection when the station alarm went off. The noise startled him so badly that he spun sideways, whacking his head on the engine compartment.

With one hand holding his head, he ran out of the launch bay into the control room down the hall. Three officers were manning the various consoles which filled the room, and at the moment each one was very preoccupied by the indicators on his equipment. Several more officers rushed in behind Jerry.

"What's going on?" Jerry asked.

A corporal at the sensor terminal, with thin-rimmed glasses and a nickname of *Peels,* was trying to make sense of the data on his screen. "We have an anomaly off the port bow."

Jerry thought nothing of the nautical reference, as the console operators, or con ops, were prone to that sort of talk. "Equipment malfunction?"

"Negative. There's something out there."

"Coordinates?"

"Multiple. It's all over the place. Like someone waving a flashlight around."

"Where is it coming from?"

"Origin appears to be . . . Earth." The con op's voice trailed off, and he looked alarmed.

The watch commander strode into the room and the duty officer looked up with a serious expression.

"Glad you're here, sir. We have an unidentified contact."

The watch commander moved over to the sensor terminal. "What is it, Peels?"

"Anomaly of some sort, sir. Coming from Earth."

"Specify."

"There's not much to go on. It registers solid but moves around like a beam of light. The thing stretches right out of the solar system, maybe out of the galaxy. It will be out of range in a few seconds."

The watch commander grabbed the communicator, trying to contact the home base in Nevada, on the North American continent. The circuits were so busy he couldn't get through, so he had the communications operator type the message by hand.

TC9810034CP4: PERIMETER COMMAND TO BASE. READING UN-IDENTIFIED ANOMALY EMANATING FROM EARTH. LENGTH UN-KNOWN. COMPOSITION UNKNOWN. PLEASE ADVISE.

The men in the control room waited quietly for a response, holding their breath in an instinctive desire not to interfere with the message. After a few minutes, one printer along the wall hummed softly and a single piece of paper dropped into the output tray. The watch commander walked over and read the message aloud.

"Base to Perimeter Command. Message received. Please stand by for orders."

He crumpled the paper and threw it in the wall disposal unit. That was it. No explanation, no recommendations, just an edict to sit on their hands.

"They don't know what that thing is any more than we do," the watch commander growled angrily. "Peels, go over those readings again and see if you can't make some sense out of them."

The watch commander walked out of the room, and Jerry returned to the launch bay, wiping his hands with an oily rag and wondering what was happening on Earth.

# CHAPTER 4

Dr. Nathan Graham was awakened from a sound sleep by the priority signal on his communicator. Stifling a yawn, he picked up the handset.

"Graham."

"Doctor Graham, this is Parkinson in Quick Response. I'm sorry to call so late, but there's been a blackout in the Denver area."

"We have standard procedures for a blackout, Mr. Parkinson."

"I know, sir, but this is no ordinary blackout. We think someone blew up the Technology Center and burned up the main power feed along with it."

Nathan was suddenly wide awake. "Blew it up! What happened?"

"Details are sketchy at the moment, but it looks like someone at the Tech Center overloaded the power grid. The main breaker didn't trip and whatever was drawing all the power exploded. The force of the explosion sent a powerhead back down the line which took out the breaker and blew a sizable hole in the street."

Nathan swallowed hard, trying not to say anything that would alarm Millie, who was awake now and listening intently. "Any casualties?"

"The reports at this point are a little vague. Several motorists were killed when the breaker blew, but there are no reports of fatalities at the Tech Center. Just a column of smoke or something sticking up through the roof and into the sky."

"What do you mean, *smoke or something?*"

"Smoke, water, metal . . . no one seems to know how to describe it. One eyewitness says it appeared out of nowhere and now it's just standing there stretching off into space."

"Are there any communications working in the area?"

"That's why I'm calling. They need you out there right away to find out what happened and make sure communications are restored as soon as possible."

"I'm on my way."

He put the communicator down and turned to give Millie the details, only to find her already up and packing a suitcase.

"What are you doing?" he asked.

"Halfway through the conversation I knew you'd be going somewhere," she said.

"You better pack your own, too. There's been an accident at the Denver Tech Center."

Millie's mouth was suddenly dry. "Ryan?"

Nathan shook his head. "Nobody knows. That's what we're going to find out."

A half hour later, Nathan was picked up by a government car and whisked away to the nearest airbase. Millie and Amie took a cab to the airport, hoping to catch the midnight shuttle to Denver. In the quiet of the cab, Millie prayed for Nathan, Ryan, the people at the Technology Center, the families of the motorists who were killed, and their own safety on the trip, as Amie dozed by her side.

Arriving at the airport a few minutes after midnight, they found the shuttle had been delayed by a sensor malfunction, a delay which Amie was convinced was ordained by God. The flight took about two hours, but only Amie was able to sleep. As they passed over the midwest United States, Nathan was on board an Army transport already on final approach to Denver; he had already drafted preliminary plans to restore communications.

The first thing Nathan noticed as the plane touched down

was a dim shaft of light against the western night sky. Intrigued but baffled, he realized he would need a closer look to learn anything else. He was met at the gate by an Army staff sergeant who drove him the twenty minutes to his hotel in an office park on the west end of town. At the front desk, Nathan found that he was already checked in, so he simply exchanged his bags for a key, and they were on their way.

He didn't really want to know what time it was; his head was already aching. The clock on the dashboard read 3:34. He asked God for strength and wisdom, and thanked Him that there weren't many cars on the road at this time of the morning.

With the power out, the sergeant was having difficulty reading the street signs, but he seemed to know the way. Nathan leaned back in his seat to try and clear his mind for a minute, and was nearly overcome by worry for Ryan. Knowing he couldn't afford to be paralyzed by worry, he sat up again and began reading the signs out loud.

"Newcombe . . . Miller . . . Kipling." The sergeant turned right and went about a block before coming to a police barricade. A police officer walked up and the sergeant opened his window.

"Good morning, officer."

"Good morning, gentlemen. May I see some identification?"

The sergeant pulled out his ID, and Nathan handed him his SAFCOM ID card. The officer took the ID cards and checked them against a roster of authorized personnel. After a moment, he handed the cards back.

"You're cleared. Stay alert in there. We have quite a few emergency vehicles coming and going."

"How is the general populace reacting?" Nathan asked.

"Mostly concerned citizens. Not much panic. Yet."

The sergeant eased his car through the barricade, picking up speed as he headed toward the Technology Center. The sergeant called ahead to let his superiors know that Nathan was on the scene. They were a quarter-mile away now, and even through the trees along Kipling Avenue they had a fairly clear view of the phenomenon piercing the sky over Lakewood. As they drew

49

nearer, Nathan understood the reason no one could describe it.

The column was constantly in motion: one minute looking like smoke from a camp fire doused with water, the next minute like boiling cream, then more in waves, like a flag undulating in the wind. The surface of the column had a dull, metallic cast at some points, but it reflected no light. The dim, silvery glow came from within.

There was another police barricade in front of the center, and the sergeant was directed to a parking area by another uniformed officer. Dazzled by the flashing lights of the ambulances and police cars, Nathan shaded his eyes for a better look.

There were charred craters everywhere, with debris strewn all over the grounds around the Technology Center. Emergency teams were carrying out stretchers and carefully depositing their charges at the end of a row of sheet-covered bodies on the far side of the lawn. Nathan felt the fear rise in his throat and prayed that his youngest son was not among them.

The car came to a stop, and Nathan thanked the sergeant and got out. Ryan was the one thought on his mind, and he knew he wouldn't be able to concentrate until he had some answers. An Army captain greeted him and led the way toward an emergency shelter set up on the front lawn of the Technology Center.

"I'm Doctor Nathan Graham. I'm here to restore communications."

"Captain Matt Foster. Glad you could make it. We need all the help we can get."

"This looks like a war zone. What happened?"

"Stuff keeps dropping out of the sky over the Technology Center. We've had over two dozen fatalities."

Nathan's stomach knotted. "Who? How?"

The captain pointed at the column over the Technology Center. "Mostly people from other parts of the country. They're just falling out of that—that column of smoke, or whatever it is. One guy popped out of it in his ground car about a thousand feet up."

"Have you had any survivors?"

"Not yet. Any fall of more than thirty feet or so is usually fatal, and most of these folks are coming in from a lot higher up. You want to hear the spooky part? One guy just steps out of that thing like he was getting off an elevator about two hundred feet up. I search his jacket and find his ID, call his home in Boston to inform his next of kin, and he answers the call!"

"That's extraordinary."

"It gets better. The birthdate checks out and everything, but I'm talking to the guy, so he can't be dead, right? I apologize for the mix-up and get off the line. Then I notice the date on the guy's license is from thirteen years ago."

Nathan was incredulous. "Time distortion. It has to be."

"That sounds like as good an explanation as any. What do we do about it?"

"We have to find out what's causing it, and fast."

They had arrived at the makeshift shelter, and the captain opened the door for Nathan. Inside, a group of five men were in the middle of a heated argument.

"We can't keep the media out forever."

"That thing is already visible for miles."

"If you just spill it to the media, you're going to have riots."

"People are going to find out no matter what we do. We need to make a statement right away. . . ."

The group fell quiet as they noticed Nathan.

"Good morning, gentlemen. I'm Doctor Nathan Graham from SAFCOM."

A white-haired man in his late fifties smiled and stepped forward, offering his hand.

"Doctor Graham! We've been expecting you. Thank you for coming on such short notice. I'm Gordon Wells, City Commissioner, and this is. . . ."

Nathan shook the commissioner's hand firmly but interrupted as politely as he could. "I don't mean to be rude, but if we could dispense with the introductions, I really need to know what we've got here."

"Oh, yes. Yes, of course. Come with me, please."

51

Gordon led Nathan to a table with an architect's drawing spread over the top.

"Here's the schematic for the Technology Center. We had a couple of surveyors out here earlier to try to pinpoint the center of that . . . thing sticking up out there. You did see it, didn't you?"

"It's hard to miss."

"Indeed. It seems to be roughly circular, and it's growing."

"How fast?"

"A few inches every hour, and accelerating."

Nathan examined the circle that had been penciled onto the drawing to indicate the circumference of the column. The data was from two hours earlier. He withdrew a mechanical pencil from his shirt pocket and drew two perpendicular lines so the circle was divided into four quarters. He put his finger down where the lines intersected and bent low to read the label.

"Who works in Laboratory Eighteen?"

"We don't know. We evacuated everyone we could from inside, but no one was asking any questions at the time. We tried the administrator at his home, but he's not answering. We thought it best not to risk going inside until we know what we're up against."

*And it's an election year,* Nathan thought. *Best not to take any unnecessary chances with the voting public so close by.* He examined the drawing again more closely.

"Have there been any attempts to determine the welfare of the people inside the Technology Center?" Nathan asked, thinking of Ryan.

"Every attempt to probe the interior of the phenomenon has been unsuccessful."

"Where's the administrator's office?"

Commissioner Wells pointed to a room just outside the circle. Nathan frowned and started toward the door.

"We'd better hurry. We don't have much time. Captain Foster? Would you like to join me?"

The captain nodded and followed Nathan. "Where are we going?"

"On a little fact-finding mission."

Commissioner Wells was right behind them. "Doctor Graham, where are you going?"

"Inside."

Nathan ignored the commissioner's protests and strode across the lawn to the glass double doors, still intact, with Captain Foster by his side. Once inside, the captain had to pull out a flashlight; even the emergency lighting wasn't working. They turned to the right past the guard station and walked down a short hallway to the administrator's office.

The door was locked, and Nathan kicked it solidly. The blow sent shooting pains up his leg but accomplished little else. The captain put a steadying hand on his shoulder and moved Nathan to one side, producing a nasty-looking handgun.

Nathan started to protest. "The door looks like solid steel. The ricochet could kill one of us."

The captain only smiled and shook his head. In the next instant, the gun went off, jerking violently in the captain's strong grip, and roaring like a small cannon. As the ringing in Nathan's ears slowly subsided, he noticed an eight-inch hole in the door above the door knob.

"Armor piercing rounds. Nice."

The captain shrugged. Nathan reached through the hole in the door and let them into the office. A brief search turned up a locked filing cabinet, so Nathan took out a small tool kit and had the lock open in a matter of seconds. His skill with a lock pick garnered a sidelong look from the captain.

"My specialty is forensics," Nathan explained.

He opened the filing cabinet and searched through the folders until he came to one labeled *Lab Assignments*. He pulled out the first set of papers and found a biography of one of the researchers, a description of the lab assigned, and a summary of the project.

Nathan was rifling for the packet on Laboratory 18 when he heard an odd sound, like water running up a pipe. Both men turned and watched in fascination as the wall of the office shimmered and disappeared, swallowed up by the advancing anomaly. Nathan cradled the folder in his arms and headed for the door.

"Let's get out of here."

Though the opportunity to collect information was enticing, the captain was no fool. "I'm right behind you."

They ran down the hall and out the front door, relieved to have escaped. Now, more than ever, Nathan was convinced of the urgency of the situation.

The two men jogged across the lawn back to the main emergency shelter and spread out the folder on one of the tables. An Army sergeant walked in with a nervous-looking gentleman in tow.

"Doctor Graham, this is Lantru Kurdisan. He has something he wants to tell you."

"Doctor Graham, I was working in my laboratory earlier today. Normally, I leave my work in the lab when I go home, but today I had something I wanted to finish at home. You see my wife has a new baby, and I need to be at home as much as possible. . . ."

The sergeant tapped his foot impatiently. "Get to the point."

"I have a cybernetic probe in my car here, which I would be willing to use, if you see any benefit from it."

Nathan addressed the sergeant. "You already tried to probe that thing, didn't you?"

"Yes, sir. We sent in wire-guided probes, robotic probes, even launched a couple of missiles with probes attached. None of them produced a single piece of data."

Nathan looked at Lantru. "How is your probe different?"

"The probe feeds information directly into my visual cortex. The images are created using a combination of sonar and thermography. My mind sees what the probe sees, but the image is monochromatic, like the image from an infrared scope."

"Sergeant, what do you think?"

"It's worth a try, sir. Our only other option at this point is to send a man through, and I can't recommend it until we have more information."

Nathan looked expectantly at the young researcher. "Mr. Kurdisan, why don't you set it up."

Lantru smiled, excited. "Yes, sir!" He turned and disappeared.

Within minutes he returned with an oddly shaped carrying case. Inside was a peculiar helmet attached to a sort of long, spindly robotic arm. Nathan and the officials from the task forces watched with interest, as Lantru configured the device and then placed it on his head, holding the arm out in front of him. Were the situation not so serious, someone probably would have laughed at him.

"I am ready. I will have to be very close to the discontinuity. I think it would be a good idea to use a safety rope and have a couple of people nearby to pull me out if I fall in."

Nathan led Lantru across the lawn, while the sergeant enlisted the help of two soldiers with the safety rope. The group assembled in front of the main doors, and then went inside. The surface of the discontinuity was advancing visibly across the hallway, approaching the lobby. Creeping along like something alive, the time distortion even looked threatening.

The soldiers tied a rope around Lantru's waist and held onto the ends as he moved slowly toward the shimmering wall of nothingness, his cybernetic probe extended. Nathan watched from behind, ready to grab the young scientist and run at a moment's notice.

As the walls disappeared into the distortion, Nathan was aware of the same liquid sound he had heard earlier. Lantru's probe was nearly in contact with the surface of the discontinuity, and Nathan tensed, unsure of what would happen next.

The probe passed through the undulating surface, and Lantru cried out. His legs went limp and he slumped forward, tumbling toward the time distortion. The two soldiers pulled back hard on their ropes, yanking Lantru's body into Nathan.

"Let's get him out of here!" Nathan yelled.

The soldiers grabbed Lantru's arms and dragged him out of the building as fast as they could. Nathan brought up the rear, looking nervously over his shoulder as if the discontinuity might be in pursuit. They took Lantru to the shelter, removed his helmet, and laid him on the floor. The probe appeared to be undamaged.

After several minutes, Lantru pressed his hands against his forehead and moaned. A medic on site had arrived and administered a painkiller. Lantru began to relax. Nathan took the medic aside.

"Do you know what the problem is?"

"I've hardly looked at him. It would be premature to make any diagnosis at this point. We need to run some tests."

"Can I talk to him?"

"Keep it brief."

Nathan knelt down next to Lantru. "Lantru, can you hear me?"

Lantru groaned.

"Lantru, it's Doctor Graham. Can you hear me? What did you see in there?"

Lantru didn't respond right away, and Nathan asked him again. When another attempt produced no response, Nathan shook him gently.

"Lantru, do you know what you saw in there?"

His mouth was moving with evidently great effort. "Doesn't make sense. . . ."

"What? What doesn't make sense? What did you see?"

"Blinding . . . blinding . . . white . . . light."

"Yes, blinding white light. And then what?"

"For just an instant . . . thought I saw. . . ." His voice trailed off again.

Nathan gripped his shoulder and shook the man a little harder. The medic gave him a warning look. "What was it? What did you think you saw?"

"I thought I saw . . . a farm."

Nathan straightened, pondering the bizarre response. The medic waved a stretcher in, and the same soldiers who had saved Lantru's life carried him out to a waiting ambulance. Nathan walked out of the shelter slowly, leaned up against the

56

outside wall and crossed his arms, trying to puzzle it out. The answer eluded him.

"A farm. Why a farm?"

He didn't have long to think, as two Army personnel carriers rolled up to the entrance and disgorged their occupants. The soldiers set up a standard perimeter, and a team of three, loaded down with equipment, approached the discontinuity. Nathan did not like the look of this and ran across the lawn to the lieutenant who seemed to be coordinating the operation.

"Lieutenant! Lieutenant! May I ask what you're doing here?"

"We have orders to blow this thing out, sir."

"Whose orders?"

"General Mardon, sir."

Nathan was irritated. He had dealt with General Mardon five years earlier, after a Memorial Day storm tore through the Denver metro area. The storm had been so severe that the governor had declared a state of emergency and imposed martial law for forty-eight hours. General Mardon was put in charge of the military police force, and thanks to his orders to "Shoot first and ask questions later," Nathan nearly had several of his work crews gunned down by over-eager squads of soldiers.

Nathan had tracked the general down the first evening and tried to reason with him, but the man was a loose cannon—a glory hog—and not one to ask permission from his superiors. After a heated exchange in which Nathan's outrage got the better of him, Nathan called the general's superiors, and used some very strong language to describe exactly what he thought of the general's tactics. The next day the general was publicly reprimanded, and the military police force pulled back on their heavy-handed tactics.

"You tell the general we don't even know what this thing is. If you try to blow it up, you may kill us all."

"I have my orders."

"Think for a minute, son. If you follow the general's orders and end up killing all the people in the Technology Center, who do you think is going to be blamed for it?" The look on the lieutenant's face showed that he knew very well who would take the blame. Nathan continued, "Wouldn't it be better to put the operation on hold and give me a chance to try to talk him out of it? That way, if he orders you to do it anyway, you have witnesses—assuming any of us survive—and he can take the blame."

The lieutenant thought it over for a moment. "Delta Team! Fall back immediately!"

The three men with the demolition gear stowed their paraphernalia and ran back to the perimeter of soldiers to wait for further orders. Nathan led the lieutenant to the main shelter and stood by while the officer put in a call to his general.

"This is Mardon."

"Lieutenant Dewitt, sir."

"Lieutenant. Is the target neutralized?"

"Not exactly, sir. I have a civilian who insists on speaking to you."

The general swore a blue streak. "A civilian? I don't want to talk to any. . . ."

Nathan cut him off. "General Mardon! General! With all respect, sir . . . *shut up!*" The sheer audacity of the statement stopped the general cold, long enough for Nathan to continue. "This is Nathan Graham."

The general growled threateningly. "Doctor Graham. I should have guessed. Still interfering with Army business, I see."

"When it is ill-conceived, yes. You don't know what you're dealing with here. Throwing explosives at it may only make the situation worse."

"I don't like self-righteous prigs telling me what to do, Doctor Graham."

"Perhaps you'd rather hear it from your superiors. You did clear this with them, I assume?" A long silence ensued, and the barest hint of a smile played at the corners of Nathan's mouth. "Ah, I see. Well, general, in that case I have a proposition for you. You postpone the demolition operation until we know what this thing is. Then if blowing it up looks like the way to go, your team can do it and we'll make sure you get all the credit."

The general hated having his back against the wall, but he knew when he was beaten. "Agreed. Lieutenant, return to base."

Nathan breathed a sigh of relief. The lieutenant terminated the connection and turned to leave, then stopped to face Nathan.

"Thank you, sir."

"You going to be all right?"

"I've worked for General Mardon for two years. I've been yelled at before."

Nathan shook the young officer's hand. "Thanks for listening."

"What are you going to do now?"

"Try to find out what we've got out there."

In the dorm cafeteria at the Space Sciences Academy on Io, Chris and Garrett were having lunch together, in another attempt by Chris to help his workaholic friend spend time away from his lab. They were halfway through when a tone sounded over the P.A. system.

"Emergency call for Garrett Alger. Please come to the comm center at once! Garrett Alger to the comm center, please. This is an emergency!"

Chris looked at his friend in shock and then noticed that everyone in the room was staring, too. Garrett stood and headed for the door, with Chris right behind. Minutes later, they burst into the Student Union Building, out of breath. A security guard was waiting and directed Garrett to the appropriate communications booth. Garrett sat down in front of the screen and saw a familiar face.

"Doctor Graham!"

"Hello, Garrett. You look well."

"Thank you. I'm doing much better since you were here. Still limping a little, but otherwise operating within specified parameters. But you didn't call to inquire about my health."

"No. There's been an incident at the New Denver Technology Center. Last night around nine P.M., MST, the power company registered two explosions, one under Colfax Avenue and one at the center. We now know that the power surge that caused the blast under the street came from the center."

"What does this have to do with me?"

"Is Chris with you?"

"I'm right here, Dad."

"Good, because this concerns you, too. The Tech Center is slowly being engulfed by some sort of anomaly—at least that's what the space administration called it—that stretches into the sky and out of the solar system. What is both peculiar and disturbing is that since this thing appeared, people *from other times* have been dropping out of it."

Garrett interrupted. "You mean people from the past or the future have been emerging from the anomaly?"

"Yes. The last object to come through was a pickup truck. It emerged from the distortion several hundred feet up and came crashing down on the lawn. From what we could gather from the wreckage, the truck may have been from another century. An hour before that, several thousand gallons of sea water came gushing out of it."

Garrett furrowed his brow. "What you're describing is a temporal discontinuity, a time distortion. But how did it happen?"

"We don't know, but according to some records we seized from the Administrator's office, the lab at the center of the discontinuity—Laboratory Eighteen—was assigned to Tatiana Rulisov. Your name was mentioned several times in her project summary."

A look of alarm crossed Garrett's face. "Rulisov!"

"Then you've heard of her?"

"She wrote me recently, requesting permission to expand on some theories of mine."

"Then you know what she did?"

"Not at all. I never gave her my consent. She wouldn't answer my letters. This is bad. This is very bad."

"Is there anything we can do?"

"Yes. Gather every scrap of information you can find about her research and arrange transportation for me and Chris."

Chris leaned further into the booth. "Dad? You said this concerns me, too. Why?"

"We think Ryan is inside the Tech Center."

"What was he doing there?"

"He came out to interview this Rulisov woman. We haven't found a trace of him yet. Garrett, we will continue trying to locate her research, and I will personally arrange for transportation. In the meantime, see if you can't discover what permutations of your work could cause a time distortion."

"I will. Good-bye, Doctor Graham."

"Good-bye, Dad."

"Take care of yourselves."

Nathan terminated the connection, thanked the Army communications officer whose station he had borrowed, and walked out of the comm shelter onto the grass beside Kipling Avenue. A chill wind blew down the street, and he pulled his coat tighter around his neck. It would be light soon.

The discontinuity appeared to have eaten up two thirds of the building now. The main operations shelter had been moved back one hundred feet, and there were more scientific and military personnel milling about.

Nathan walked into the shelter and found his Quick Response Team from SAFCOM, as well as the city officials he had met with earlier. Representatives from the media and the military were also present. He briefed them on his conversation with Garrett, but the conversation quickly degenerated into an argument about public relations and crowd control. Giving up for the moment, Nathan took his team to one side for private instructions.

"Osbourne, I want you to work closely with the power company to restore communications. We can use the military generators for now, but the people of Lakewood need to know what's going on. We need to do everything we can to avoid panic in the public. If you can have them up by noon, that would be great."

"Noon? That's going to be pushing it."

"Then push it. We need it, ASAP. Patterson, contact Perimeter

Command. Have them send their fastest ship to the Space Sciences Academy on Io to pick up Garrett Alger and my son, Chris, and bring them to Earth. Captain Foster tells me we have the authority of the Joint Chiefs of Staff. Code Baker Baker Delta."

Patterson nodded slowly, obviously taken with the level of authority he had been given. Nathan fixed him with a look that said *Don't let it go to your head,* and Patterson loosened back up a little.

"How do I contact Perimeter Command?"

"Start with the IPF Command Base in Nevada. Ask for Commander Griffen. Tell him what's going on, and use my name. He knows me. Michalson, you come with me. We have some detective work to do."

At 0600 hours, Solar Mean Time—which was the normalized time for space stations across the solar system—the entire platoon at Perimeter Command was called into an emergency meeting. Nearly one hundred men—pilots, officers, and mechanics—squeezed into a moderately-sized briefing room in the space of ten minutes.

Women were not assigned to Perimeter Command because exhaustive studies had shown that stationing men and women together on remote, often dangerous, assignments increased the incidence of violence and accidental death among the men. Those same studies showed that a mixed group that was able to achieve unity, was often more closely knit than any single gender group; but the bureaucrats had decided that the risks outweighed the benefits.

Jerry Wysoski stood at the back of the group in the briefing room fidgeting, trying to wipe various rocket motor fluids off his hands with a filthy rag. The watch commander stepped to the front and addressed the group.

"Seventeen hours ago some yoyo actually created a temporal rift over the western United States. This was the same anomaly we picked up yesterday on our sensors. Apparently some elected official is pretty desperate, because Base Command has ordered us to dispatch the LX44 and proceed at extreme velocity to the Space Sciences Academy to pick up two passengers for immediate transport to Earth. I'm looking for a volunteer."

One of the pilots raised his hand. "A volunteer? You mean no copilot?"

"The LX44 is a tight squeeze, even without passengers. I'm afraid this one's a solo. Anyone want to play nursemaid for a couple of academy brats?"

Jerry stopped wiping his hands and looked up. "What are the names of the passengers?"

The watch commander checked his roster. "Alger and Graham."

"I'll do it," Jerry shot back.

The watch commander's face broke into a broad grin. "Well, burn my boots up. Our head mechanic wants a pleasure cruise."

The room rippled with laughter. Jerry was well-liked by everyone in the room, primarily because he worked on the engines—and it never pays to be at odds with your mechanic. He looked around the room and smiled disarmingly.

"I'd do almost anything to get away from you bulkheads for a few days."

Laughter erupted again, and the pilot standing nearest to Jerry slapped him on the back, knocking the wind out of him. The watch commander restored order.

"If there are no objections, it looks like this little milk run falls to Mr. Wysoski."

There was a general murmur of approval from the group, and somebody yelled, "Hey Jerry! Say hi to your brats for me." Another followed up with, "Don't forget the diapers!"

Jerry gave the second man a thin-lipped smile. "Now there's a man who's begging for some engine trouble."

The man grinned and threw up his hands in surrender. He wanted to be absolutely sure Jerry knew he was only kidding.

Nathan had spent most of the morning trying to find someone who knew about the computer setup at the Technology Center. Michalson went through the information taken from the administrator's office, looking for clues that might lead them to the right person.

Power had been partially restored to the area, with Osbourne's expert help. But since the main computer had been swallowed up by the discontinuity, Nathan's only hope was that there was a backup system somewhere that might contain information on Rulisov's research.

Starting with a name given to him by Michalson, he began calling employees of the Tech Center, getting additional numbers as he went along. At one point, he had to put the communicator down and laugh. It occurred to him that this was almost as difficult as setting up a social event at church.

After quite a few calls, he finally talked to a researcher who told him the main computer was linked to the mainframe computer at the Federal Center down the road. Nathan commandeered a driver and several moments later arrived at the main gate of the Denver Federal Center. After a brief explanation to the guard, he was directed to the building that housed the computer center.

He left the driver with the car and ran inside, explaining again the purpose of his visit to a receptionist. Immediately he was ushered into a conference room and moments later a middle-aged man with thinning blond hair and blue eyes walked in.

"Doctor Graham? I'm Geoffry Buswald, Director of Computer Services. I understand you have an explanation for all the commotion down the street."

"I do. It seems one of the experiments got out of hand and created a temporal distortion."

Mr. Buswald pursed his lips. "That's a new one on me. I assume you are referring to that odd column adorning the Tech Center." Nathan nodded, and Mr. Buswald continued, "How can I help?"

"We need information on the project that started this whole mess, and I understand your mainframe might have just what we are looking for because it was connected to the Tech Center mainframe."

"It was. Please follow me."

Mr. Buswald led Nathan through a maze of hallways to the computer center. Once inside, he directed him to a smooth, beige, plastic box about the size of a small washing machine. As Nathan watched, he sat down at a terminal next to the box.

"What was the name of the researcher?"

"Rulisov."

Mr. Buswald typed in some commands. "The file is here, but I can't access it. Apparently the link is still open. If the main computer over there is inside this temporal distortion, as you call it, chances are it was stopped in midtransmission."

"Meaning?"

"Both systems are equipped with numerous backup, shutdown, and failsafe mechanisms. Most disasters—power outages, earthquakes, tornadoes, even bombings—give a few nanoseconds' lead time. This gives the computer time to terminate the transmission and send an abnormal termination code. Needless to say, a temporal distortion is not on your usual disaster recovery list. The code was never sent, so the link remains open."

"Then we can't access the data?"

"We could cut the line, but chances are the data you need most would be lost. We need to send a shutdown code from the other end. Then the file will be closed properly."

"Is that easy to do?"

"If you can reach the main computer, yes. The line itself is twenty feet underground. Dig it up and you still risk severing the line."

"Where does the line exit the Technology Center?"

"In the basement, I think."

"That may be our best chance."

Mr. Buswald grabbed a scrap of paper and scribbled a string of alphanumeric characters.

"Here's the shutdown code for the main computer. You'll need a few other items, too."

He rummaged in a nearby cabinet and pulled out several bits and pieces of hardware.

"Here is a remote keyboard and a hacksaw with a nonconducting blade. You'll notice the cable leading from the keyboard has a spike at the far end. Once you've used the saw to cut down to the insulating layer, stop cutting and insert the spike into the cable with one smooth thrust. Type in the shutdown code, and you're done."

He handed the items to Nathan, who looked a little surprised. "That's it? It sounds too easy."

"It should be. I have to stay here and mind the shop or I'd come and do it myself. If you need me, here's my emergency number."

Mr. Buswald scribbled on another scrap of paper and stuck it in Nathan's shirt pocket. Nathan thanked him, and his host explained how to get back to the lobby. He was eager to try the remote keyboard, so he wasted no time in making his way back to the waiting car. They drove swiftly back to the Technology Center.

At the emergency shelter he found Millie and Amie waiting for him. They were wearing jackets and sipping hot cocoa. Nathan walked over, kissed his wife, and put his hand on his daughter's head.

"I take it you've checked in at the hotel. What are you two doing here?"

Millie took another sip of cocoa. "We almost weren't. I had a terrible time convincing the policeman that we needed to be in here. What have you learned about Ryan?"

"Very little, I'm afraid. At least he's not among the casualties."

Millie breathed a sigh of relief. "I hope we find out something soon."

"Actually, we're working on the problem right now. I'm glad you're here. I may need your help. We're trying to shut down the main computer link so we can access some remote data."

"Sounds interesting. At the very least it will keep us busy."

Off in a corner of the tent, an Army colonel and one of the city planners were engaged in quiet discussions. Just then, a private ran through the entrance looking white as a sheet. He ran up to the colonel and saluted.

"At ease, private. What is it?"

"NAVSAT report from flight com, sir. We've left orbit."

"Come again?"

"The Earth has left its orbit around the sun. They traced it to the discontinuity, sir. Apparently when that thing appeared, the Earth was jerked out of orbit somehow. USGS registered a massive gravimetric fluctuation in the Earth's mass, as if—for just a millisecond—the planet weighed only a few thousand pounds."

"That's incredible! How far out are we?"

"Only a few degrees, but the global temperature is already dropping."

Nathan, who had overheard the entire exchange, turned to Millie and Amie.

"We'd better work fast."

He walked outside and stopped in his tracks. It was starting to snow.

## CHAPTER 5

Squeezed into the cockpit of the LX44, Jerry Wysoski was blazing through space at .6 of light speed. The ship was designed for speed alone, which made it an ideal courier ship. This particular ship was a revised prototype, built by the Japanese and on loan to Perimeter Command for testing.

The seat was a little too small and the cockpit cramped; but there was an expandable rear compartment which slept two more or less comfortably, so the accommodations were tolerable. He was still trying to get used to the controls, which were slightly different from the controls in the old IPF Fighters.

He was four hours out from Perimeter Command, with twenty-six to go, and he wanted to be sure he could handle the ship before he had to put her into orbit. One of the test pilots had warned him not to exceed .85 of light speed, but he had offered no explanation other than a vague reference to the ship "acting funny."

An answer like that only served to stimulate Jerry's curiosity, and he soon found himself nudging the stick forward and watching the velocity indicator. The pilot was as good as his word, for shortly after Jerry hit .85 the ship began acting very funny indeed.

Tiny white flames danced over the skin of the ship. The cockpit suddenly was elongated and was filled with a reddish haze. He looked down and saw his hand still wrapped around the control stick, his arm impossibly long, as if it were made of rubber.

Jerry eased back on the stick, and immediately the flames and haze were gone, and the cockpit snapped back to normal. He took a deep breath and let it out slowly, as the pounding in his chest subsided.

*Okay,* he thought to himself, *I guess we won't try that again.*

It was evening at the Space Sciences Academy, and Garrett Alger sat alone in his lab, poring over his theories on Subtemporal Irrelativity. He had decided to try to replicate the discontinuity using a chronospatial modeling program on his computer, but no matter what he attempted, he was unable to produce anything like what Dr. Graham had described.

Perhaps the most interesting result was in response to a string of random variables he keyed in out of frustration. The computer analysis reported that the solar system would collapse in two hundred eighty days, and all humanoid life in the galaxy would be transformed into cabbages.

Garrett laughed, remembering the old "garbage in, garbage out" adage from his early programming days. He had taken himself very seriously back then, and probably would have found little humor in a population of cabbages.

The door opened soundlessly, and Chris Graham walked in. "Hi, Garrett."

Garrett jumped and gave Chris a nasty look. "Didn't your mother ever teach you to knock?"

"Sorry, but I have some important news. Perimeter Command is sending a ship to pick us up. It should arrive about this time tomorrow."

"Excellent. I must say, when your father arranges transportation, he doesn't fool around."

"No, he doesn't. Have you had any luck with your models?"

"No. So far, everything about these equations seems to be very stable."

"You want to break for a cup of coffee?"

"No thanks. This is really irritating. I want to figure it out."

"Don't knock yourself out."

"Actually, that's not a bad idea. It's about the only thing I haven't tried."

He typed for a moment and hit the Enter button. Chris peeked over his shoulder to see what the computer thought of a universe without Garrett Alger.

"I don't see any change."

"I was afraid of this. I could die tomorrow and the universe wouldn't even notice."

Chris patted his friend on the shoulder. "I would, so try and get some sleep, you big lunkhead."

"Thanks, Mom. I'll do my best."

Chris smiled and left the room as quietly as he had come in, and Garrett leaned forward, preparing to go over the equations one more time.

Neither one of them slept very well that night: Garrett because he was preoccupied with his computer models, and Chris because he was worried about Ryan. Under the best of circumstances Chris never slept very well on the eve of a trip.

Garrett spent the balance of the next day putting all his scientific projects on standby. Chris made the rounds of his professors and begged for permission to go to Earth, promising to catch up on his studies within a week of his return. Only two professors gave him any trouble, but both reluctantly acquiesced when he explained that Garrett had requested his presence.

Chris met Garrett that evening in the observation lounge for Shuttle Bay Number 2. Exhausted, he dropped his small duffel bag next to Garrett's on the floor and collapsed in an empty seat.

"You look terrible."

"Thank you. I feel terrible. And you look worse than I feel."

"Any luck with your computer?"

"I managed to destroy the universe by galactic convergence, but that was mostly because I wanted to see what it would look like. Still no evidence of temporal distortion."

The landing lights in the shuttle bay came on, and they watched through the huge Plexiglas window as the LX44 dropped soundlessly onto the landing pad. As the bay doors closed, and the room began repressurizing, they could hear the engines idling. Grabbing their bags, they made their way into the airlock, waiting for a green light.

After a few moments, the door opened automatically with a slight hiss, and they entered the landing area, looking the ship over with admiration. A ramp extended from the back of the ship, and the pilot walked down and stood with his arms folded and a broad grin on his face.

Chris's mouth dropped open. "Jerry!"

"Hey, preppie."

"What are you doing here?"

"When I found out you were one of the passengers, I volunteered. Are you going to introduce me to your friend here?"

"Oh, sorry. This is Garrett Alger, Destroyer of Universes."

Jerry shook Garrett's hand warmly. "Garrett, huh? You don't hear that name every day. Charmed to register your face, G-man. I'm Jerry Wysoski, Saver of Grahams."

"Saver of Grahams?" Garrett asked.

"Jerry saved my life about a year ago, and he's never let anyone forget it."

"Actually, I saved his whole family," Jerry boasted, his grin widening.

Chris shook his head, as one would over a reprobate uncle. "Still the modest introvert, I see."

"How else can I get any respect? Now, if you fresh-faced cadets are through socializing, we'll frag this big ball of pizza."

Without another word, Jerry strode up the ramp and into the ship as if he owned it, leaving Garrett staring at Chris with a puzzled expression. "Frag this big ball of pizza?" he mouthed silently to his friend. Chris thought for a moment and then realized that from orbit, the surface of Io *did* look a little like pizza topping.

"I think he means 'leave Io.'"

"Ah."

Jerry's voice came from inside the ship. "Hey, Rellycinders

and your sistyugly! Your pumpkin awaits! You want to be late for the ball?"

Garrett and Chris walked up the ramp, through a very short passageway, and squeezed into the back seats of the cockpit. After a minute of twisting and straining, they were strapped in, but their knees were jammed up nearly against their chests.

"Um, we're not going to ride like this the whole way?" Chris asked hopefully.

"As I recall, the order was to deliver you alive. But before you get your hopes up, this thing barely sleeps two, fully loaded."

"What does *fully loaded* mean?"

"Two dwarfs and a backpack."

"I was afraid of that."

Jerry finished the prelaunch sequence, closed the ramp, and fired up the engines. A peculiar thrumming sound caught Chris's attention immediately.

"What kind of engine is that?"

"It's a beefed-up version of the Bussard/Osaka Ramjet."

"I thought that was still in development."

"It is. This is one of two working prototypes."

Garrett, who had never cared for space travel anyway, was not thrilled by this piece of news. "Wonderful. Well, you made it this far, and it hasn't fallen apart yet."

Chris was dreadfully curious. "How does the engine work?"

"No one's been able to explain it to me in words I understand. There's some gizmo inside that reduces inertia, I think. But she's fast."

"How fast?"

"Nobody knows. After point-eight-five of light speed you start getting some zany Einsteinian effects. Doppler distortions, little white flames—you know, mass to energy kinds of stuff."

"Incredible."

Garrett cut in. "Yes, but let's not try it, shall we?"

Jerry smiled and addressed the communicator. "Spaceport Control, this is the LX44. We're good to go."

"Roger, LX44. Repressurizing."

72

The bay doors opened overhead, revealing a glorious canopy of stars. The speaker came to life again.

"You are cleared for takeoff. Watch your wings."

"I know. It's a tight squeeze. You secured for vertical takeoff?"

"All sensors show secure."

Jerry smiled like a little kid, punching in the vertical thrusters, jerking back on the control stick, and engaging the main thrusters in almost the same motion. The ship was suddenly vertical, and blasted out of the launch bay like a rocket. He could have used his emergency thrusters, but that would have blown open every access panel in the shuttle bay, and probably done some structural damage to the walls as well.

The LX44 traced a spiral arc up and away from the surface of Io, hurtling toward the gaseous clouds of Jupiter. The ship dipped down near the tempestuous wisps of orange and white, veering away at the last minute in a steep power turn, and finally settling into a vector toward Earth.

Garrett tilted his head back and shut his eyes tightly, trying not to be sick. Chris felt his face must be an unhealthy shade of green, but he was determined not to embarrass himself by throwing up on government property.

Garrett took several deep breaths. "I strongly suggest you not do that again, unless your objective is to discover what I had for dinner."

"Sorry about that. I thought you landlubbers might need a little adventure in your humdrum lives. So many months with your nose in a book can cause your brain to atrophy."

He dropped the temperature in the cockpit a few degrees and increased the flow of oxygen, and his passengers began to feel better immediately. Garrett tried to sit forward, thought better of it, and decided to keep his eyes closed for a bit.

Chris was beginning to feel he would keep his dinner down after all. "You could have warned us."

"Yeah, but then you would have tried to talk me out of it, and I would have had to do it anyway."

A long silence ensued, during which Jerry adjusted the controls and prepared to engage the autopilot. Chris turned around and loosened his safety belt.

"You've heard of the *Jesuit Rule,* Jerry?" Chris asked.

"Nope."

"It's better to ask forgiveness than permission."

"Sounds like words to live by."

"Yeah. Or die by."

Jerry smiled and nodded, conceding the point. He didn't have much opportunity to indulge in philosophical discussions, and found them a pleasant diversion when they arose.

"People who don't ask permission have more fun," he countered.

"They also get spanked more often. Something tells me you didn't get your hand slapped much when you were little," suggested Chris.

"No. I got my clock cleaned. I'll tell you about my dad sometime. He had a killer left hook."

The note of bitter irony in Jerry's voice made Chris sorry he had touched on such a painful memory. He decided to change the subject.

"So, Saver of Grahams, do you ever get tired of the view when you're flying?"

Jerry paused for a moment to think up an appropriate response. "Well, Champion of the Insipid, the answer is, in a word—yes. One of God's gifts to humankind is an astonishing ability to adapt. The down side is that we get used to awesome beauty much too quickly. Take this view for instance. In an hour, we won't even notice it."

"Yes, but in two, we may notice it again."

"True."

Garrett opened his eyes and looked past Jerry at the vivid expanse of stars. Praising God for His creation was a relatively new thing for Garrett, but the view out the front made it easy. The depth of black with its manifold pointillism of luminous radiance was breathtaking.

"'He counts the number of the stars; He calls them all by name,'" quoted Garrett.

"What's that from?" Jerry asked, looking out the window.

"The book of Psalms," Garrett answered.

"Which one?"

"One hundred forty-seven. Fourth verse, I think."

"You read the Bible much?"

"For a few months there I studied it quite a lot. I hope to do so again, if my schedule ever lets up."

Jerry engaged the autopilot and operated the controls which caused the area behind the cockpit to expand. When the walls had finished moving, the room measured eight feet wide, ten feet long, and six feet high. Under other circumstances, the effect would have been claustrophobic, but when faced with the alternative of days crammed in the cockpit, it seemed like a presidential suite.

Once they had each staked out a place on the narrow beds along the wall, Jerry looked at them with a serious expression.

"So tell me what this time distortion is all about. My commander made it sound like a joke. It isn't, is it?"

Garrett shook his head. "Definitely not."

Chris ran his hand through his hair, wishing they knew more. "We don't even know how dangerous this is. It could be anything from a tourist attraction to the collapse of the universe."

"That sounds a little extreme."

"Until we know more, we have to consider the extremes as possibilities," Garrett replied.

"Can you stop it?"

"That's what we're going to find out."

The news that Earth had left its orbit spread quickly across the face of the globe, catapulting the City of Lakewood to the center of international attention. Even in crisis, city officials bemoaned the fact that they couldn't turn this into a public relations bonanza.

As the temperature dropped, populations across the globe began to panic, and countries began to place their military on alert. A consortium of world leaders was hastily formed for the dual purpose of keeping the peace and finding a solution to the bizarre dilemma.

Scores of media people, would-be saviors, and the curious streamed into Denver by air and land. Throngs of people crowded the police barricades day and night, hoping for a better view of the discontinuity, an interview, or just an audience with the people in charge. More National Guard troops were called in, but keeping order was growing more and more difficult with the freezing conditions and a general air of mass panic.

Spaceports were closing worldwide as a result of the colder temperatures, especially those not equipped for such weather. Though a few wealthy families managed to charter last-minute flights to the Martian Colony, for most people there was no escape.

At the center of it all, because he had taken decisive action early on, Nathan Graham found himself quite by accident in charge of the crisis. He had coordinated with the Army the setup of a perimeter around the area, including forward monitoring stations for minute-by-minute updates on the time distortion, and had laid out a plan for getting into the Technology Center. The attempt failed—due to their target entrance being swallowed up by the distortion—but the people who had gone with him nominated Nathan as the leader, and the city commissioner immediately seconded the motion.

Emergency response people, scientific observers, even military personnel were all coming to him for instructions. At the moment Nathan was in the main shelter (which had been moved across the street to the front lawn of the hotel), to brief a group of White House staff, military advisors, and scientists. Nathan stepped calmly to the front of the gathering.

"Approximately one hour ago, we tried to enter the Technology Center to break the computer link with the Federal Complex down the road. Because of the expansion of the discontinuity, all routes to the basement have been cut off. The link is still active, and as long as that is the case, we have no way of retrieving the information we need."

Nathan described the way the systems were attached and the

necessity of a controlled shutdown to avoid losing critical data. The group began discussing options, while Millie and Amie listened from a corner of the shelter. Amie was studying the plans for the Technology Center intently.

After ten minutes of brainstorming, the best idea anyone could come up with was digging a hole into the basement of the center. Unfortunately, preliminary calculations indicated that the hole would be finished about fifteen minutes after the building had been completely swallowed up by the discontinuity.

As the hubbub of conversation continued Amie walked up to her father and tugged on his jacket. "Daddy?"

"Not now, sweetie."

She tugged more insistently. "Daddy!"

Nathan was irritated. "I said, not now."

"It's important."

Nathan took a moment to get control of his temper, then turned around and faced his daughter. "What is it, Amie?"

"I think I can get into the basement."

"How?"

"Through the ventilation ducts. Come here, I'll show you."

Nathan walked over and looked at the drawing while Amie pointed with her finger. "Right here. See? There's a shaft right down to the room where the cables go out of the building."

He couldn't believe his eyes. They had completely missed it because the duct was too narrow for an adult. No one had considered sending a child.

"You're right. You could get in right here, crawl about thirty feet, down ten feet and you're there."

Millie stood up and looked over her husband's shoulder. "You're not seriously considering sending her in there?"

"She's the only one around who can do it. You know I wouldn't even think of it, if the situation were not so serious. Besides, I'm more confident of her abilities than most of the people in this room. Present company excepted, of course."

Millie exhaled in frustration. Every bone in her body wanted to protest, but she knew that Nathan was right and that the situation was getting worse by the minute. If they missed this chance to cut the link and get the necessary information, they might all be doomed.

"Well if it has to be done, let's get it over with."

Suddenly Amie was the center of attention, as she was hastily fitted with a makeshift backpack and tool belt. She removed her heavy jacket and put on instead a couple of sweaters. She was incredibly relieved that she had worn pants instead of a skirt. With a coil of rope over her shoulder, she was ready to go.

Nathan explained how to cut the cable and insert the spike from the remote keyboard, and then had her repeat the instructions back to him so he was sure she understood. As she recited the details perfectly, he was struck afresh by how sharp and levelheaded she was. He made a mental note to thank Millie for all her hard work spent raising their daughter.

He put the keyboard in Amie's pack, the slip of paper with the shutdown code in her pocket, and attached the nonconducting hacksaw to her tool belt, which already sported an assortment of screwdrivers and wrenches.

They went over the route to the basement once more, then headed outside. The temperature was in the low twenties, so the task force had been issued arctic jackets. Everyone she passed seemed to know who she was and what she was doing, which made her feel important. Complete strangers were waving or patting her on the back and wishing her well.

Millie had asked to come along, but propriety demanded that she stay behind. With such an important task, it wouldn't do to have it appear that Mommy and Daddy were seeing their little girl off on some childish adventure.

Nathan and Amie picked their way across the icy street carefully, as vehicles on emergency business passed through the barricades. They waded through kneedeep snow to the left side of the building, finding a grate set in the wall right where the plans said there should be one.

Nathan pulled a screwdriver off Amie's belt and went to work on the grate. His knuckles were aching from the cold by the time he finished the task. He looked at his daughter and smiled.

With her tool belt, backpack, and rope, she looked like a mountain climber.

He put his hand on her shoulder and closed his eyes. "Dear Lord, please protect Your servant Amie. Surround her with Your angels, and keep her safe. Give her wisdom and please get her in and out of there as quickly as possible. Crown her efforts with success, for Your glory."

Amie nodded in agreement. "Amen."

She handed her dad one end of the rope and crawled into the ventilation duct, playing the rope out behind her as she went. With the backpack, it was a tight squeeze, even for her, but she found she could scoot along fairly quickly by keeping her head and shoulders down.

Fifteen feet in, it was pitch black and she had to pull a small flashlight off her belt to continue. In less than a minute, she was at a dark hole in the floor of the duct. She called over her shoulder.

"I'm at the shaft."

Outside, Nathan coiled the rope around one arm, grasped it tightly with both hands, and braced himself. "I'm ready," he called back.

The passage continued beyond the hole, so Amie climbed over, dropping the rope down the hole and feeding her legs down after it. As her waist passed over the edge, she reached behind her for the rope, twisting awkwardly to grab it with both hands. She let herself down hand over hand, and in a few moments her feet hit bottom.

She squeezed her body and scrunched down until she was on her hands and knees in the basement level duct. Pulling out the flashlight again, she felt her stomach tighten. The light showed only smooth metal as far as she could see. With some effort she shone the light behind her and twisted around so she could see.

The rope was still hanging reassuringly in the shaft, and beyond lay the grate she was looking for. She backed down the duct until the grate was in front of her. The light from her flashlight revealed a storage room.

One push on the grate sent it clattering to the cement below, much to her relief. The floor looked pretty far down, but not far below the opening was a freestanding shelving unit that looked fairly sturdy. Tucking the flashlight in her belt, she slipped her legs through the hole, turned over on her stomach, and stretched her feet toward the top shelf of the unit. Contact.

Her footing was shaky at best, and she began earnestly looking for a way down from her swaying perch. Climbing down was out of the question, and jumping didn't seem like such a great idea, but it was beginning to look like her only option. Without any warning, from the far side of the room came the sound of water rushing down a pipe. She turned to look, and the sudden motion caused the shelving unit to tilt away from the wall and come crashing down onto the cement floor, taking Amie with it.

She lay curled up on the cold floor, stunned by the impact. She was sure her arm was broken. But amid the pain and waves of nausea, all she could think was how stupid she was for not being more careful. She gritted her teeth and groaned, determined not to scream.

"Lord, help me!"

The pain subsided a little and she was able to sit up without passing out. This was definitely not part of the plan. She squeezed her eyes shut and yelled with all her might.

"Daddy!"

The sound of her voice seemed to go nowhere, absorbed by the glimmering, amorphous wall which was slowly moving toward her. She was thankful for her father's explanation of the discontinuity, as it was the only thing keeping her from panic. Time was running out, though. Groping for the flashlight with her good hand, she wrestled it loose from her belt and flashed it around the room.

A few feet to her left, she saw the computer conduit. She worked her way to her feet and stumbled over to the wall, steadying herself with her good arm. The pain was almost unbearable, and she had to breath through her nose with her teeth clenched to keep from throwing up. Taking the hacksaw off her belt, she cut into the conduit until she could see the insulation inside.

The next part was going to be a problem. Trying to get the backpack off over a broken arm might make her pass out, and if that happened, she knew she was finished. She reached over her shoulder with her good arm, strained and grasped the keyboard, and hauled it out. Holding it between her legs to get a hold of the cord, she grabbed the spike and jammed it through the insulation into the conduit.

She had no way of knowing if the connection was good, but she couldn't worry about that now. She shifted her weight to put the keyboard down so she could type, and it slipped from her grasp. Instinctively she tried to catch it with both hands. Gut-wrenching pain shot through her arm, and she fainted.

# CHAPTER 6

When Amie came to a few minutes later, she didn't remember at first where she was. She shook her head gently to clear it and turned to check on the progress of the shimmering wall of the discontinuity. It was already halfway across the room.

Every movement now caused her pain. Even something as simple as retrieving the scrap of paper from her pocket was nearly impossible. She took several deep breaths to stave off a bout of dizziness and concentrated on the characters scrawled on the paper. At least the pain was helping her not to panic.

Amie laboriously typed the characters one by one on the keyboard and hit the Enter key. That was it. She stood to leave and nearly fell over the shelving unit lying on the floor. Her ungraceful entrance to the room had left no way of escape, and the contents of the shelves were scattered all over the place.

By using one arm and putting her back to it, she was able to stand the unit upright again. Knowing the shelves would fall right over if she tried to climb, she looked for something to steady it. A full trash can by the door was the only thing big enough to be of any use. The distortion was now so close there was barely any room to maneuver. She dragged the trash can in front of the bookcase, imagining the icy tendrils of the anomaly creeping up her back.

Using her good arm, the trash can, and the shelves, she

managed to scramble up into the ventilation duct, just as the trash can disappeared into the void. She tucked her legs inside in panic and worked herself around until she was standing upright in the shaft.

The pain was a dull throbbing now, and Amie knew enough to realize she was going into shock. In a foggy haze of pain and exhaustion, she saw that there was no way to climb back up. She thought about giving up, but the idea of quitting was intolerable. She wrapped the rope several times around her waist using her good arm, and put all of her fear and frustration into one tremendous scream.

"Da–ddy–y–y!"

Outside in the snow, Nathan heard the cry for help. His heart leaped and he tugged on the rope. Amie felt like dead weight, and he feared the worst. Saying a silent prayer, he sat down and braced his feet on either side of the hole in the wall, and pulled for all he was worth.

Using her feet to keep her back against the wall, Amie rose up the shaft very quickly, and pitched forward at the top into the ground level duct. The shooting pains up her arm were continual now, and she wondered when it would all end. With her remaining strength, she held on, her knuckles turning white, and then she was out. Nathan helped her to her feet and then saw her injured arm.

"Can you walk?"

"I think so, but can't I just rest for a minute?"

"I'm sorry, sweetheart. We have to get out of here."

The same, strange, liquid sounds Amie had heard in the basement came from the ventilation duct, and Nathan recognized it as the sound he had heard in the administrator's office. He put his arm around her and they took off as fast as they could for the street.

The snow hampered their progress considerably, and Nathan heard the sound again. He looked back to see the remainder of the Technology Center slowly disappearing into the discontinuity. Fifty yards to his left, the two technicians he had assigned to the forward monitoring station were showing no signs of leaving. Nathan let go of Amie and took several steps in their direction.

"Hey! Fall back! Fall back!" he yelled.

One of the men looked up and waved, and they began breaking down the equipment in a hurry. Nathan turned around to collect Amie and found that she had continued on without him. She was barely conscious, her legs churning automatically. She was almost to the street.

"Amie!"

Across the street, scientists and technicians were buzzing excitedly. The computer was working and it was clear they would be able to access the Rulisov research on the Federal Complex mainframe. Outside the main shelter Millie was straining for signs of her husband and daughter when she saw Amie about to stumble blindly into the street.

In a heartbeat, Millie took off at a dead run across the lawn, shouting Amie's name as she went.

At the same moment, Nathan was yelling at Amie from the other side, hobbling through the snow in a vain effort to catch up with her. To Amie, it seemed that suddenly the whole world was yelling her name, and the voices were an annoyance—a distraction from her one goal of finding a place to lie down.

She staggered into the street. Forty feet away and coming too fast was a truck carrying collapsible emergency shelters. The driver stomped on the brake and the wheels locked, but the truck just kept coming, sliding on the ice. Nathan was still too far away to intervene, but Millie was at the curb.

Too late, she saw the truck. With superhuman effort she reached Amie and pushed as hard as she could. As the truck slammed into Millie, Nathan covered his eyes reflexively and screamed. "No!"

Chaos broke out across the street. Several bystanders yelled for medics while others ran toward the road to render assistance. Nathan saw Amie lying beside the road, and he yelled for the paramedics. He ran over to his daughter, found she was still breathing, and then moved out of the way to make room for the emergency team. They stabilized her quickly and prepared her for transport.

*Millie.* Only a few feet away, she lay on the ice, looking as if she were asleep. Nathan elbowed his way through the crowd, and for one desperate moment, he thought she might be all right. Then he noticed the paramedics shaking their heads. He knelt down, taking her limp hand and holding it to his chest.

There was nothing he could say, nothing he could do. His emotions sealed themselves off in shock, and his intellect took over. He knew Millie would have wanted him to look after Amie, so he stood up and walked back down the street and saw her safely into the ambulance. He asked the driver where they were taking her and said he would follow shortly.

The crowd of onlookers, all people he had been working with for the past several days, were watching him now, some with pity, some with uneasiness. Would this tragedy cause him to abandon them? Nathan walked over to the truck. The driver took one look at his face and began backing away, but to his surprise, Nathan only began giving orders to clear the machine out of the way. Millie was already loaded into an ambulance.

Nathan turned on his heel on the ice, pulled in three directions. *Millie. Amie.* But to abandon the project now could result in catastrophic loss of life, maybe even the end of the world. After wrestling with himself mightily for a moment, he climbed into the ambulance and it drove off.

There was work to be done, but it would have to wait until he took care of his daughter.

As the LX44 cruised through space, Garrett sat on one of the bunks reviewing the reports Dr. Graham had sent him before they left the academy. Jerry was in the middle of telling yet another story from his brief glory days as an IPF pilot.

"There was this cadet named Lumquist. He was a real hammerhead, with thick glasses—no offense, G-man—and a bad attitude. One day we get a distress call from a freighter and he's on deck, ready to make a big impression on the watch commander. He jumps into his fighter and gives the thumbs up, only he hits his retros by mistake. Vroom! Right through the back wall of the launch bay."

Chris held his sides, laughing. "Was he hurt?"

"Just bumps and bruises. The ship ended up in the officer's mess, so you might say he made a big impression on the watch commander. Everyone called him *Lumpy* after that. Actually, he turned into a pretty nice guy once his ego was out of the way."

"Well, they say 'Pride goeth before the officer's mess.'"

Jerry nodded. "A little humility goes a long way. I should know. Some of my best friends are humil. Hey, G-man? You're awfully quiet over there. What are you doing?"

Garrett looked up from the sheaf of papers he was holding. "I've had no luck replicating the discontinuity mathematically, so I was hoping to find some clue in the eyewitness accounts that would explain what it is."

"So, what is it?"

"I don't know."

Chris leaned over to look at the papers, and Garrett handed them to him, leaning back to take a break. Chris read with great interest about the recent happenings in the city of Lakewood.

"People falling out of the sky? Vehicles? This is incredible. Why haven't you been reading this to us?"

"I was rather enjoying Mr. Wysoski's tales of adventure."

"Wait a minute, this one has a police report. Attachment number six. Whoa! This is amazing. Some guy falls hundreds of feet to his death. They check his ID, call his house, and he answers. Turns out his ID is thirteen years old."

Garrett frowned and leaned forward. "Say that again?"

"Turns out his ID is thirteen years old."

"No, before that."

"They call his home and he answers?"

Garrett pointed at Chris. "That's it!"

"What's it?"

"She split the time stream!"

Chris was in the process of switching from having fun to serious thinking, and it wasn't always an easy transition. "What are you talking about?"

"Don't you see? If the man left this time stream thirteen years ago by falling through the discontinuity, he shouldn't be there to answer the communicator now."

Jerry sat up from his lounging position, for the first time really interested. "You really think this guy came from another time stream?"

"It's the only explanation that makes any sense at the moment."

"But if the time stream is split, how do you know which one is the right one?"

"We don't. But at least it gives us a place to start."

Several hours after the accident, Nathan returned from the hospital. Amie was in a coma. The doctors were doing all they could, but with a state of emergency in the city, business was very hectic in the critical care facility.

In the end, Nathan decided the best way he could help Amie was to try to make the time distortion go away. It would be pointless for her to survive the accident only to freeze to death in a few weeks. With Earth's new orbit the temperatures were heading far below zero.

After praying over her and committing her to God's care and protection, he returned to the main shelter and found a communications officer to try to get an outside line. He wanted to inform Garrett that Rulisov's research would be available upon his arrival and find out if there was anything that needed taking care of in the meantime. The comm officer was having no luck and didn't seem to care much, either.

The door burst open suddenly, and several military personnel walked in with the city commissioner in the lead.

"Nathan! This communique just came from the Central Intelligence Agency. It's from the Chairman of the European Commonwealth. He says that at this time tomorrow, the commonwealth will launch two Class-B Devastator missiles, targeted for Lakewood. He does not mean this to be an act of hostility, but hopes to destroy the discontinuity before Earth's orbit decays any further. As this action will also destroy most of Colorado and portions of adjacent states, he strongly recommends that citizens who can leave the area do so within the next twenty-four hours."

Nathan tried to take in the magnitude of the situation. "What was the President's response?"

"Outrage at first, but he doesn't have a better alternative. Panic is spreading. People are willing to try almost anything."

"I see."

Nathan walked over to the communications console and put his hand on the operator's shoulder.

"Let's try once more. And this time, work as if your life depended on it."


Back on the LX44, all was quiet. Chris and Garrett were asleep on the beds; Jerry had managed to wedge his body between them and was sleeping on the floor. When the emergency message signal sounded, it took him the better part of a minute to extract himself from the narrow space between his two sleeping companions.

He fought his way to the cockpit and slid in the pilot's seat.

"This is LX44 en route to Earth. What's the nature of your emergency?"

"LX44, this is Doctor Nathan Graham on Earth. Do you have Garrett Alger on board?"

At the sound of Nathan's voice, Garrett and Chris were up and on their feet. Jerry thumbed the communicator again.

"Doctor Graham! It's Jerry Wysoski. Garrett was asleep, but he's on his way."

"Jerry! It's great to hear your voice. We're going to need all the help we can get on this one."

Garrett leaned over Jerry's shoulder. "Nathan, it's Garrett. What's happened?"

"The Chairman of the European Commonwealth is threatening to bomb Denver in an effort to destroy the discontinuity. Since we don't have any facts, we have no way of proving that this is not a good idea."

"I guarantee you it is not a good idea, but I can't explain why at the moment. I need to talk to the chairman directly. Can you arrange that?"

"It will take some doing, but I'll try. Keep the channel open."

The communicator went silent, and Garrett pulled out a notepad and began scribbling furiously. After several minutes, Nathan came back on.

"Garrett, I have the chairman on the line. Chairman, this is Garrett Alger."

The chairman spoke perfect English. His voice was well modulated and he sounded as if he were in his mid-fifties. "So you are the one who is responsible for all this?"

"I suppose I am, sir, at least indirectly. I implore you, sir, please do not introduce any explosive devices into the time distortion. The sudden application of high energy to temporal phenomena can produce unpredictable results."

"Such as?"

"Without knowing the exact nature of the experiment which created the phenomenon, I was only able to perform some preliminary calculations. Both scenarios are pretty grim, I'm afraid. The first shows the force of the blast being redirected and tearing away half of Earth's atmosphere."

"Interesting. And the second?"

"The second shows the force of the blast channeled into the discontinuity, tearing apart the fabric of space/time entirely."

"So your recommendation would be that I postpone launching the missiles?"

"Unless your intention is to destroy either the planet or everything living on it."

"What do you suggest as an alternative?"

"I will be on Earth in . . . ," he looked at Jerry, who held up two fingers, "two days. If I am unable to come up with a solution shortly thereafter, we'll try it your way."

The communicator was silent for a moment, then the chairman was back on. "I am not convinced. When you arrive on Earth, we will meet. If I remain unconvinced, I will carry out my original plan twenty-four hours after our meeting."

"Thank you, sir."

"Good luck, Mr. Alger. I will see you in two days."

The speaker was silent. Jerry was about to close the channel, when Nathan's voice came over again.

"Garrett, it's Nathan. We got Rulisov's research."

"Excellent. What was the nature of the experiment?"

"She was trying to push a small block of lead two minutes into the future, using an antigraviton emitter."

Garrett was impressed. "Antigravitons? How did she stop the decay?"

Nathan was in over his head. "I don't understand the question. Here, let me find someone who can help."

There was a long pause. Chris looked at Garrett with some of the old hero worship he used to feel.

"Did you really come up with those scenarios while you were waiting to talk to the chairman?"

Garrett looked down at his notes sheepishly. "Not exactly. I just established that it was theoretically possible to produce those kinds of results. Of course, with math it's theoretically possible to do just about anything."

Chris smiled accusingly. "You lied."

"I extrapolated."

"You prevaricated."

"I exaggerated. I didn't want some foreign bureaucrat playing Russian roulette with the Earth."

The speaker came to life again, startling them both.

"Garrett, this is Doctor Lionel Merrick from Lawrence Livermore Laboratory. Doctor Graham tells me you have a question about how Miss Rulisov stopped the antigraviton decay. She used a positron field to stabilize the antigravitons."

Garrett nodded. He was beginning to understand. "How big was the lead block?"

"Just under two inches."

"The power curve must have been enormous."

"Logarithmic. It looks as if she used an industrial strength capacitor. Our guess is she calibrated the system to take all the power she could get. When the main breaker failed, she got a lot more than she bargained for."

They talked for another twenty minutes about the mechanics of Rulisov's equations, with Garrett taking copious notes. At one point, Jerry looked at Chris and rolled his eyes, but they kept quiet, not wanting to interrupt such an important flow of information.

When they were finished, Nathan came over the channel. "It's Nathan again. Jerry, do you have a SATREC facsimile machine on board?"

"Sorry, Nathan. This flight is strictly no frills. Even if we did, most of the satellites have either left orbit or crashed by now. I'm having enough trouble just following your trajectory."

"I was hoping to send this material to Garrett."

Garrett cut in. "I'll be there in two days. Have a team of fifty ready to help—people like Doctor Merrick. Engineers and technicians, too. I will need a fully equipped lab with qualified assistants and metallurgy capabilities, access to a supercomputer, and hard copies of all of Rulisov's research."

"Doctor Merrick is nodding, so I assume he understands what you need. No promises, but we'll do what we can. Is Chris with you?"

"I'm here, Dad."

There was a long pause. "I hate to deliver bad news this way, but I think you need to know."

Chris didn't like the sound of his Dad's voice. "What is it?"

"Your mom and your sister were in an accident. Amie's at the hospital in a coma."

"What happened?"

Nathan's voice faltered, and he choked down the tears and

regained control by sheer effort of will. "Amie walked in front of a truck. Your mom pushed her out of the way just in time. Amie hit her head when she fell."

"Where's Mom?" Chris asked, fearful of what the answer would be.

"She didn't make it. They tried to save her, but she had massive internal injuries. She never regained consciousness. I'm sorry, Chris, to have to tell you like this."

Chris felt a mixture of shock and anger. He was angry at Amie for being so careless, angry at his mom for not saving herself, and angry at Nathan for giving him the news at all. Tears welled up in his eyes, but then it occurred to him that he wasn't the only one who was suffering.

"I'm sorry too, Dad. I'll be there soon."

He pushed the communicator button, terminating the connection, and made his way to the back corner of the room. He knew that hanging up on his father wasn't the right thing to do, but he couldn't think of anything to say. Somehow, in the first shock waves of grief, it was hard to be philosophical. Deep down, he knew the Lord would work everything out, but it hurt too much to think at the moment.

Chris put his face between his knees and wept, his body racked with sobs. Garrett and Jerry gave him as much space as they could, both wishing there was something they could do to spare their friend.

As the discontinuity grew, the emergency response people were having to move the shelters more frequently. They were now set up on the far side of Addenbrooke Park, as the time distortion was already encroaching on the Rianna Hotel.

Nathan stood in the main shelter, barking orders into a communicator like a field commander. He knew if he stopped working for very long, the pain and grief would be overwhelming. He was determined to press hard until the end of the crisis came, one way or another.

The temptation to submit to denial, to let himself believe that Millie and Amie were all right and it had all been a dream, was very strong. Nathan refused to take that route, and instead set all familial thoughts and emotions aside, with a mental note *To be dealt with later.* He understood that he couldn't keep up the charade for long, but he prayed it would be long enough to finish the race set before him.

With Dr. Merrick's help he kept on trying to line up the people and resources Garrett had requested. He was finding it increasingly easy to enlist support as the temperature continued to drop. The pattern of the sun across the sky kept changing. There seemed to be a universal understanding that the end of the world might be at hand.

By midnight he had picked a team of twenty-five top scientists, due to arrive by noon the next day, along with a score of technicians and mechanical engineers. The equipment was scheduled to arrive no later than the following evening, which was an impressive deadline considering the weather conditions.

He slept in the shelter that night, not wanting to sleep alone at the hotel surrounded by his wife's things. He asked God for His mercy on Amie, and then for peace. A few minutes later, he fell into a shallow, restless sleep.

Morning dawned cold and cloudless. The sun rose in the north and began its bizarre trek southeast across the sky. The days were now only six hours long, with the temperature well below zero in the sun. Work during the daylight hours was critical.

By late morning, a makeshift laboratory had been assembled at the far edge of the park, along Garrison Avenue. The forest service generously provided a dozen snowmobiles for travel between the monitoring stations, the main shelter, and the laboratory.

During the night, the discontinuity had encompassed the front half of the Rianna, expanding at a rate of one foot per ten minutes. The area of distortion was now several hundred yards across and visible from thirty miles away.

Scientists worldwide were trying to unravel Rulisov's equations, but without a fundamental understanding of Garrett's work, no one was having much luck. A group at MIT began collecting and correlating data as it became available.

By the end of the day, all of the people and equipment were in place, awaiting only Garrett's arrival. Almost everyone was aware of Nathan's fragile emotional state, but for the moment the task at hand was allowing him to cope with his pain. He was providing invaluable leadership, so no one broached the subject of the tragedy with him. Some therapist would have to sort it all out later.

Chris woke to find Garrett still asleep and Jerry already scrunched into the pilot's seat. Chris's eyes were red and puffy, but at the moment he felt no emotion at all, just a dull ache. He walked forward and leaned into the cockpit.

Jerry had a star map in one hand and was busily scrawling equations on his pant leg with the other. Chris watched for a minute.

"Hi."

"Morning, preppie."

"We have paper in the back."

"Not . . . ," he wrote some more figures, ". . . to worry. This ink is water soluble."

"Why aren't you using the computer?"

"We're not getting telemetry. I'm trying to figure out where Earth is going to be in about six hours, so we don't miss it by a million miles."

"Don't let me interrupt."

Chris walked back to his bed and sat down. Garrett never budged as Jerry finished his calculations and punched them into the navigational computer. The autopilot processed the new information, and the sound of the engines changed slightly as the course adjustments were made automatically.

Jerry came back and sat down next to Chris. "I got a status report from Earth while you were asleep. Things look pretty bad. Global temperatures are falling below zero. Whole populations are freezing to death along the equator. Conservative estimates give the planet about two weeks."

Chris stared at Jerry and shook his head. "I can't believe this is happening."

Jerry jerked his thumb in Garrett's direction. "Can the G-man really make this thing go away?"

"If he can't this whole trip's going to be for nothing."

Three hours later, they picked up telemetry again, this time from a ground station on Earth, and the LX44 homed in on the North American continent. As they came in on approach, Jerry received landing coordinates from the ground, but he hardly needed them. Even from space the discontinuity was visible, like a long, gossamer thread stuck through a bowling ball.

While Chris and Garrett took their seats, Jerry cut their speed to 7500 miles per hour and dropped down into the atmosphere. Flames engulfed the ship as it lost altitude, but the hull was designed to take the heat, and they continued their descent.

Jerry skimmed through the upper atmosphere over the North American continent, crossed the Atlantic Ocean, and dropped into an approach vector toward Europe. The Chairman of the European Commonwealth was headquartered in Paris, in the State of France, and Jerry requested permission to land on the lawn in front of the Capitol Building near the Arch of Triumph on the Champs-Elysées. Permission was granted and he dropped a few thousand feet of altitude, cutting his speed to 600 miles per hour.

Chris had never been to Paris, and he thought it a shame they wouldn't have time for sightseeing, though he was hardly in the mood. The city came into view ahead, and the first identifiable landmark was the Eiffel Tower. The small room at the top of the tower still contained the furniture and personal effects of Alexandre-Gustave Eiffel, who designed the tower for the Paris Exposition of 1889. Chris wondered what Alexandre would have thought of the sight of the LX44 sweeping out of the Parisian sky on a frigid Saturday afternoon.

Jerry maneuvered the ship to a standstill hover over the lawn of the Capitol Building, and then slowly brought her down until the landing struts touched down on the snow. A half dozen men in overcoats ran across the lawn, carrying jackets, and waited for the passengers on the ship to debark. It was 15 degrees outside, so Chris and Garrett welcomed the jackets offered them by their hosts. Jerry decided to tough it out, and by the time they reached the steps into the Capitol Building, he was slapping his arms trying to keep warm.

The Capitol Building was relatively new, but city ordinances had required that it be built to blend in with the exquisite architecture of the rest of the city. The architects who designed the building had used an expensive technique to fabricate the simulated hand-hewn stone for the facade. Even a stone mason would have had trouble proving the building wasn't hundreds of years old.

The new arrivals were led through the vaulted oak halls of the first floor to a palatial office at the far end. Immense double doors opened inward, revealing thick burgundy carpet and dark wood furniture beyond. A pair of smaller double doors opened at the far end of the room, and the Chairman of the European Commonwealth emerged, wearing a very unfriendly expression. He walked up to the unwashed visitors standing in his receiving area and looked them over. When he had finished his examination, he turned to face Garrett.

"Mr. Alger, I presume?"

"Yes, sir."

"Come and sit down."

Chris and Jerry sat on a small antique sofa, and Garrett took an ornate, high-backed chair upholstered with leather. The Chairman sat opposite Garrett with his back ramrod straight.

"As you are no doubt aware, the situation has deteriorated since we spoke."

"I know, sir."

"Mr. Alger, do you see that man over there?" The chairman pointed to a short, balding man in a drab suit, seated along the wall with a briefcase chained to his wrist.

"Yes."

"If, at the end of our meeting, I am not satisfied with your explanation of the problem, I will give him a signal, and he will open his briefcase and press a button, launching two Class-B Devastator missiles targeted for Lakewood, Colorado."

Garrett flushed. "But you said you would wait twenty-four hours!"

"I have changed my mind. The situation is too serious. So tell me. Why should I not launch my missiles in an effort to destroy this time distortion of yours?"

Garrett wished for a moment that he had charts, graphs, maps—anything to help try to get his point across. Since none of those things was available, he would just have to make the best of it. He looked around the room, hoping to find something he could use for a demonstration. Along one wall was a table with refreshments, including several pans with hot food in them. Garrett stood up and walked over to the table.

No one stopped him, but the chairman and his officers watched with considerable interest as Garrett collected a stack of cloth napkins and two of the heating cannisters from underneath the pans. He walked over to a small table and set everything down, dragging the table to a spot between his chair and the Chairman's.

Garrett sorted the napkins into two even piles of five each and turned to one of the uniformed soldiers standing by the door. "May I borrow your laser pistol?"

The soldier looked questioningly at the chairman, who nodded, and then handed his pistol to Garrett.

"Mr. Chairman, you are thinking in a linear fashion, which accounts for our current misunderstanding. You are thinking of blowing out the time distortion as one might blow out a tornado or an oil well fire."

Garrett took one of the heating cannisters, sealed it, wrapped it in a napkin, and put it on top of the left pile of napkins. Setting the laser pistol for a narrow beam, he fired into the napkin. A tiny hole burned through the cloth, and the cannister blew open with a small explosion, tearing a hole in the napkin and scattering the left pile across the table.

"In this case, the target for the explosion is above the surface, and the force of the explosion is focused on the target object."

Garrett held up the napkin that had been on top of the left pile. Beyond a few black smudges, the cloth was undamaged. "The surface beneath the target was largely unaffected."

Garrett took the entire right pile of napkins, wrapped the remaining heating cannister inside, twisted the ends into a bunch, and pulled out one of his shoe laces to tie the packet together. Taking careful aim, he fired again. This time the explosion was more muffled, but the bundle of napkins flew off the table and tumbled across the floor. Garrett retrieved the smoldering package, untied it, and held up the napkins. All but the outside one had charred holes through the middle.

"The phenomenon over Lakewood, Colorado, is neither a tornado nor any other naturally occurring artifact of the weather. It is a twisted, folded rip in the space/time continuum—a junction or intersection between multiple time streams. If you detonate an explosive device inside it, or even near it," Garrett held up the charred remains of the napkins, "you will very probably tear apart the fabric of space/time itself."

The chairman looked thoughtful for a long moment, and then signaled to the little man with the briefcase. The man stood up and walked out of the room. "You have made your case, Mr. Alger. It seems that you are our only hope to put an end to this madness. Please go. We are running out of time."

Garrett looked at the chairman for a moment, to see if he were trying to be clever. The man's face was expressionless. Bowing slightly, he turned to Chris and Jerry, and the three of them walked back down the hallway to the entrance. They all had the feeling they had narrowly avoided disaster, and no one wanted to say a word until they were safely back on the ship.

The same six escorts walked them back across the lawn to the LX44, and Chris and Garrett returned their jackets before walking up the ramp. Jerry followed them in, closed the hatch, and squeezed himself into the pilot's seat. After a quick call to the nearest traffic station, he was cleared for takeoff.

The LX44 soared up into the afternoon sky, headed for

North America. Once they reached cruising altitude, Jerry broke the silence.

"That was close."

Their speed was such that they were only at cruising altitude for a few minutes. Shortly after crossing into American airspace, Jerry dropped altitude and speed and made a wide turn around Colorado to come in from the West. The mountains and the plains were completely covered with snow. He brought the ship in low over the front range of the Rocky Mountains, swooped over the treetops of suburban Lakewood, and touched down in the middle of Addenbrooke Park. The landing struts sank into the snow, and he switched off the engines.

"It's minus ten degrees out there, gents. I hope you brought your long underwear."

Of course, in the rush to leave, neither one of them had packed much in the way of warm clothing. Fortunately, they were met at the bottom of the ramp by a group of people dressed for frigid weather and carrying arctic jackets. The threesome donned the jackets, and the entire group hurried over to the main shelter. Once inside, the hoods came off, and Chris recognized one face immediately.

"Dad!"

Chris threw his arms around Nathan, and then stood to one side so his dad could make official introductions to the staff. With that task complete, Nathan turned to Jerry.

"So, are you headed back to Perimeter Command?"

"Actually, I'd like to stay on. If you think you can use me."

"I was hoping you'd say that, but you may be signing your own death warrant."

"I know, but how many times do you get a chance to save Earth?"

Nathan smiled. "Well said. Mr. Alger? If you feel up to it, there is a lab full of people awaiting your command."

He turned Garrett loose on the lab, leaving Jerry to watch the proceedings, and walked with Chris back to a private shelter that had been assembled for his personal use. The shelter was ten feet square with two cots and not much else, but it was warm and much preferable to the outdoors.

Nathan poured two cups of hot chocolate from a thermos and handed one to Chris, and they removed their jackets and sat down facing each other on the cots.

"I'm sorry things happened the way they did," Nathan ventured hesitantly.

"It's not your fault."

"It is my fault. Amie was nearly delirious. I should have been watching her more closely. None of this would have happened if. . . ."

Chris put his hand up. "Don't. Please." Tears misted his eyes, and he squeezed them to stem the flow.

Nathan put a hand on his son's shoulder. "It's all right. God is still in control." The words sounded hollow, but he knew they were true.

"It's hard to believe it right now."

"I know. You have to decide to trust." Nathan stood up and handed Chris his jacket. "Come on."

"Where are we going?"

"To see your sister."

They walked to the parking area near the road, and Nathan arranged with the sergeant in charge of the motor pool to take one of the military vehicles equipped for snow travel. Nathan fired up the engine, and Chris turned the heat on full. Abandoned vehicles lined both sides of the road; some of them had been moved with a bulldozer. Chris couldn't escape the feeling that they were driving through a demilitarized zone.

They turned off Kipling onto Colfax and drove twenty blocks down to Wadsworth. Nathan was not surprised at the absence of traffic. The weather was terrible, and the snowplows were having trouble keeping the roads clear. Every few blocks, Chris was able to catch a glimpse of the skyscrapers downtown, over the snow-covered shops.

"Why are the lights off downtown?"

"The power companies are trying to keep power going to the

communities. The governor has declared a state of emergency, and all businesses are closed."

They took Wadsworth to 38th Avenue, and turned left. A few blocks up on the left was Lutheran Medical Center. Nathan turned into the main parking lot and parked at the curb. Most of the cars in the lot had been there quite a while, judging from the depth of the snow on the roofs.

Chris got out of the car and sank in snow up to his thigh. "Yuck. I like snow as much as the next guy, but this is ridiculous."

They waded indoors, and shook most of the snow off near the entrance, then made their way through the lobby to the elevators. Makeshift beds were packed three abreast down every hallway they passed, and there were clearly not enough doctors to go around. Chris followed his dad onto the elevator, and Nathan pushed the button for the basement.

"They put Amie in the basement?"

"I thought we should see your mom first."

"I'm not sure I'm ready for that."

"You may not get another chance. You need to say good-bye."

Chris leaned back against the wall and took a deep breath, trying to steel himself for what was coming. Nathan led him down the hall to the temporary morgue and spoke quietly with the attendant. He let them into the viewing room, and disappeared through another door, reappearing a few minutes later with a table on wheels. The body on the table had a sheet over it, and Chris caught a glimpse of rows and rows of similarly shrouded forms in the large room beyond the door.

The attendant took his leave, and Nathan pulled the sheet back from the face on the table. It was Millie. Other than a lack of color in the cheeks, she looked as if she were sleeping. Chris caught himself listening for a breath, and sighed.

"Good-bye, Mom."

There wasn't anything else to say. The last time he talked to her, he had told her he loved her. He knew she knew it. Now she was in God's hands. Chris walked out, and Nathan called for the attendant.

"Thanks."

Amie's room was on the fourth floor. There were six other patients crammed into the small space. Nathan squeezed between the beds until he stood next to his daughter, and Chris came around to the other side of the bed. She looked so small with the long tubes in her arms and huge bandages around her head. Nathan took her hand and held it, not saying anything, then he turned and walked out of the room.

Chris sat down on the bed, trying not to disturb the tubes, and put his hand on top of hers.

"Hey, Squirt. It's Chris. I heard you weren't feeling so great, so I came all the way from Jupiter just to see you. What do you think of that? Things are getting pretty interesting here. But I guess you knew that already. Of all the silly things to do. How many times have I told you not to lead with your face? I wonder what Ryan would say if he could see you right now. He'd probably say the same thing. I love you, little sister. Always have, always will. I'm sorry I wasn't here to look out for you, but I know you understand. I'd tell you to get better, but the way things are going, you may be better off where you are."

Chris used his thumb to wipe the moisture away from the corners of his eyes. "Listen, I gotta go, but we'll come see you again real soon. Take care, Squirt."

There was no sign of a response.

Chris joined his dad out in the hall. "Let's go."

They drove back to Lakewood in silence and returned the vehicle to the motor pool. The visit to the hospital had been hard, but Chris knew it was necessary. He hoped he would be able to go see his little sister again, hopefully after a good night's sleep.

Back in their private shelter, Nathan took a long breath and let it out slowly, stretching out on the cot. Chris noticed for the first time how bone weary his father looked. Obviously he hadn't slept well for days. Now there was a lull with Garrett's arrival, but Chris knew from experience that if his father relaxed too much, he was going to get sick.

"Don't let down too much, Dad. There's still plenty to do around here."

Nathan closed his eyes. "Don't worry. I'll just take a little nap. We can go check on Garrett's progress in two or three. . . ." He was already asleep.

This particular day at sea was calm, and warm—at least for this time of year in the Gulf of Alaska—and nothing in the weather reports suggested tomorrow would be any different. Not that the weather was much of a concern for a ship the size of the supertanker *Cyprus*. Over a half mile long, weighing millions of tons fully loaded, the gargantuan oil carrier could pretty much ignore anything the sea wanted to throw at her.

Up in the captain's cabin, Jonas Christos sat at his desk, studying a nautical map. This was not the kind of sailing that made him happy to be a captain. Bad weather, rough seas, even a near collision would have been preferable to the monotonous smooth ride the crew had been enjoying for the last two days.

Christos could only assume the crew was still on board. He hadn't seen anyone since the ship left port. With a crew of eight, making a run they had made a hundred times before in a ship with most of its functions mechanized, there wasn't much need to disturb the captain.

It was with some surprise, therefore, that Captain Christos received an urgent call from his first mate.

"Captain, there's something off the starboard bow!"

Christos walked out of his cabin onto the deck. Off the starboard bow less than a mile away was something bizarre-looking. A water spout, perhaps. He ordered the pilot to turn the ship toward the water spout, so he could get a better look. Then he noticed that whatever it was, it extended out of sight into the sky. Like a column of mercury. The closer the column came, the larger it looked.

The captain called the pilot and ordered an emergency turn to port. The supertanker groaned and started into a slow left turn, and to the captain's horror, the column moved toward the ship. He could see that sea water was being sucked into the void inside the column, which had now moved into the ship's path.

A frantic call to the pilot stopped the engines, but the tanker continued drifting forward.

Christos watched grimly as the bow of his ship disappeared into the void. Panic rose in his throat, but he couldn't deny an undercurrent of curiosity beneath the fear. Whatever this phenomenon was, he was about to see it firsthand.

# CHAPTER 7

The first thing Garrett did when he walked into the lab was to kick everyone out, sequestering himself with Rulisov's research. Somewhat abashed, the scientific and technical personnel retired to their shelters to await further instructions.

As evening came, Nathan slept on, and Chris did not disturb him. Unable to rest himself, Chris took a brisk walk to the main shelter. It was nearly empty, the only warm body in the place being the communications officer. Chris walked over and sat down next to him.

"Keeping busy?"

The comm officer snorted. "Yeah, right. About every three hours I make a status report to headquarters and that's about it. Most of the comm lines are down. I can't even find out how my family is doing."

Chris shook his head sympathetically. The comm officer took another look at him.

"Hey, aren't you Dr. Graham's kid?"

"That's right."

"I'm really sorry about your mom."

"Thanks. She did what she had to do."

"Yeah. I guess we all are."

The relative quiet of the shelter was shattered by a horrendous cacophony of screaming metal and a violent bucking of the ground beneath their feet. Chris was bounced off the ceiling but managed to roll when he hit the floor, sustaining only cuts and bruises. He picked himself up off the floor, holding his ears against the aftershocks of the noise and trying to keep his balance. The ground continued to undulate underfoot as he staggered out of the shelter. Nothing in his experience could have prepared him for the sight of a wrecked supertanker lying on its side in the middle of Denver.

The ship had emerged from the discontinuity a thousand feet up and toppled end over end into the neighborhood below. A score of houses—all previously evacuated—were splintered in an instant, crushed flat by the enormous weight of the supertanker.

Rivers of dark crude oil poured through the ragged gashes in the vessel's hull, and the superstructure at the rear of the ship burst into flames. The flash flood of petroleum flowed downhill, following the low canyons and ravines west of the discontinuity, inundating the surrounding community, the Federal Center, and Kipling Avenue. Due to a quirk of the terrain, most of the oil coursed north of Addenbrooke Park, so the shelters of the emergency response teams were spared.

The flames on the rear of the ship intensified for a moment, then there was an explosion. A plume of fire lit up the night sky, and the surrounding oil ignited. What followed was a conflagration worthy of a world war, as the burning oil set fire to the houses still standing, and the Federal Center.

All around the camp, people ran out of their shelters to witness the spectacle of a city on fire. There was nothing to be done. The buildings that were burning were devoid of people, and all the firetrucks in the state would not have made a dent in the holocaust. In the absence of immediate danger, the only thing left to do was look.

Chris started toward his father's shelter and met Nathan halfway there.

"Are you all right?" Nathan asked, concerned.

"I was thrown around pretty good, but I'm okay."

"We'd better check on Garrett."

Nathan and Chris hurried as fast as they could through the

snow, across the field to the mobile laboratory. The lab had originally been a square, one-story building set up on stilts, but the building now sat at a shallow angle, most of the stilts bent or broken off. Chris found the front door and had to grasp the hand rail to enter because of the tilt of the short stairway.

Inside, only the emergency lights were working, casting strange shadows around the debris in the room. The equipment was going to need replacing.

"Garrett! Are you in here?" Chris called out.

"Over here."

Chris and Nathan worked their way to the place where the voice had come from, but the shadows of the ruined machinery made it difficult to see.

Chris peered into the dark. "I can't see you."

"Then please stay where you are. You're almost standing on my hand."

Chris looked down and caught the pale outline of Garrett's fingers. "Can you move?"

"Yes, but I don't think it's a good idea. The last time I tried, something heavy started sliding this way."

Nathan moved over to one of the emergency lights, detached it from the wall and carried it over to Garrett's position. Several pieces of battered machinery were balanced precariously on a broken table, all of them tottering over Garrett's head. His leg was pinned by a file cabinet wedged under the table.

Nathan set the light down on the floor in such a way that it illuminated the area. "Chris, let's move that stuff off the table before we do anything else."

While Nathan stood ready to catch anything that fell, Chris picked up each of the pieces of equipment from the table, and set them down out of the way. With the immediate threat removed, Nathan held the table, which allowed Chris and Garrett to push the filing cabinet aside. Garrett stood up gingerly.

"Ow!"

Chris put a steadying hand on his friend's shoulder. "Looks like you thumped your knot pretty hard."

The cut on Garrett's forehead wasn't deep, but there was already a lump forming and his head throbbed.

"Thanks for your help. What happened?"

"A supertanker just blew up part of Lakewood."

Garrett's mouth slowly dropped open, and he walked past the Grahams to the door. The fires from the spilled oil were still burning out of control, and the charred carcass of the ship was visible in silhouette against the crimson inferno beyond. The lights in the lab came on suddenly, as some industrious electrician restored power to the camp, and Garrett closed the door.

They spent the next half hour cleaning up and putting the lab back in order. Garrett tested the equipment and found only two machines that weren't working properly. One of the devices was made usable by switching to a built-in backup circuit, but the other would have to be replaced.

Nathan took his leave, but Garrett asked Chris to stay for a few minutes. He pulled out Rulisov's charts and lab workups and spread them on the table. After thumbing through the notes for a few minutes, he found what he was looking for. The page contained some arcane references in English and several series of mathematical equations, consisting of symbols Chris did not recognize, except for a few letters from the Greek alphabet.

Chris glared at Garrett. "You know this stuff is gibberish to me."

"Me, too."

Chris was stunned. "Gibberish? You? But she used your equations."

"Yes, but these are permutations I never anticipated. Look here. She has inverted the ratio of mass to energy conversion, reversing the gravitational constant."

"Is that possible?"

Garrett frowned. "No. But I have been unable to locate her error."

"What was she trying to accomplish?"

"Time travel. Movement of inert matter through the time continuum. Look at the two series of equations. The first one is fine, establishing the mass to energy coefficient of a two-inch cube of lead, and the differential between the exponent and the first term in the discriminant for the. . . ."

"Right," Chris said, cutting him off.

Garrett got the message and continued. "Sorry. The second is correct up to this point. Then she has this equation, to which the solution is the reversed gravitational constant, but the solution is incorrect."

He rummaged around in the stack of papers again, finally producing a hand-drawn diagram of some kind of mechanical device. Garrett put the new page next to the one with the equations and studied them intently.

"This is a working diagram of the temporal logic circuit she constructed for her experiment. These equations on the left have to do with the power requirements, corresponding to the first series on the other page. The temporal logic circuit was supposed to regulate the flow of antigravitons through the positron matrix, so that every atom of the lead cube would move forward in time together. If the atoms moved at different rates, there was a possibility that the object would disintegrate."

"Done right, would this thing work?"

"I don't know. Theoretically, maybe. You are aware of the principle that time slows down as gravity approaches infinity? I believe she was trying to localize the opposite effect by concentrating antigravitons on her target object. If the opposite of the time/gravity principle holds true, time should speed up for the object, and it should move forward in time. It's just a theory. There are probably a hundred reasons why it wouldn't work."

"So what actually happened? Did she split the time stream like you said?"

"I'm sure of it, but I don't know how. I've been over these equations a hundred times and I still can't find the cause."

Chris looked out the window at the reddish glow from across the field. "I hope you find it before any more large objects come through."

Garrett followed Chris's gaze for a moment and then froze. Something was nagging at the back of his mind. The ship should never have come through. No one in his right mind would. . . .

"Chris, I need your help to think something through."

"Shoot."

"Let's assume that every intersection of the discontinuity with a time stream manifests itself in the same way. If you were the captain of a supertanker in the middle of the ocean, and you saw the discontinuity sticking up out of the ocean, what would you think it was?"

"I don't know—probably a water spout or something."

"What would you do?"

"Go and have a look, I suppose."

"Right. So you're headed toward this anomaly at sea, and as you get closer, you see that it isn't a water spout at all. In fact, it's unlike anything you have ever seen before, and it's big. What would you do then?"

"Try and get away from it. Fast."

"So you give the order and your ship changes direction. End of crisis."

Chris was intrigued. "But then the ship wouldn't have come through."

"Exactly. What could have caused the ship to come through?"

"Maybe the captain panicked, or he had a heart attack."

Garrett was not convinced. "Perhaps. Are there other alternatives?"

"Equipment failure, operator error—it could be anything."

Garrett shook his head. "Actually, it can be very few things. You have named several possibilities, but there is another. What if the ship was not moving?"

"Then the discontinuity would have to move."

"What could cause the time distortion to be drawn toward the ship?"

Chris smiled. "A fondness for crude oil?"

"Its mass. The ship represented a large mass in close proximity to the distortion. My guess is the captain tried to escape, and the distortion followed."

Garrett returned his attention to the two pages on the table, scrutinizing them as if they would give up their secrets by the

110

sheer force of his will. Then he slapped his palm down on the table. "That's it!"

Chris was so surprised by his outburst he nearly fell out of his chair. "What?"

"The antigraviton emitters were shot through a positron matrix, remember? Look at the temporal logic circuit. The last section is a graviton generator. Do you know how a graviton generator works?"

Chris thought for a moment. "Like a collector. It pulls gravitons from the largest mass in close proximity. In this case, the Earth."

Garrett smiled. "Don't you see? When the power surge hit the system, there was a burst of antigravitons ten trillion times more powerful than has ever been produced in a laboratory. The force of the antienergy split the time stream and momentarily sucked away Earth's mass—which threw Earth out of orbit and started the rotation toward the new poles. Earth's graviton imbalance corrected itself a moment later, and since Earth was the source for the graviton generator, the supply of energy to the rift is virtually inexhaustible."

"But what does that have to do with the supertanker?"

"When the antigravitons come through the far side of the positron field, they revert to gravitons again. But the positron field now extends to the edges of the discontinuity, so all the energy inside is antigravitons, with a graviton shell. That's why the time distortion registers solid, even though it has no measurable mass. Since gravitational bodies are attractive, the graviton field of the discontinuity was drawn to the graviton field of the supertanker. Like magnets. You get them too close, they stick together."

Chris looked dazed. "What do we do now?"

Garrett scrutinized the diagram once more. "We have to shut off this machine."

The next morning, the sun didn't come up at all, due to the peculiarity of Earth's rotation. About ten o'clock, Garrett emerged from the lab and called a briefing in the main shelter.

Obviously, he had been up all night. His clothes were rumpled and his hair spiky from running his fingers through it in concentration. With the key team members assembled, he drew a piece of notebook paper from his pocket and placed it on the table in front of him.

"As most of you know, Tatiana Rulisov was attempting to push a lead block into the future to demonstrate time travel as a viable possibility. The foundations for her research included a number of incorrect assumptions based on some of my previous work. The machine she constructed was flawed in its concept, and to make matters worse, she calibrated it beyond the trip voltage for the main power feed.

"We don't know why the breaker didn't trip, though residue from inside the remains of the breaker box suggests that something was wedged in with the breaker. Had the experiment gone as planned, there would have been a small rift in the space/time continuum which would have sealed itself immediately. Instead, the system was subjected to a tremendous increase in power which we now believe split the time stream."

A young scientist up front raised his hand. "That shouldn't be possible, assuming temporal inertia to be a fact."

"Quite correct. However, by stablizing antigravitons in a positron field, she in effect created an inertial dampener. Space/time was fed through itself and split dozens, maybe hundreds of times. Imagine taking a paper napkin—or in this case, a stack of napkins—and feeding one corner of it through the center. If you pull it all the way through, theoretically it will be inside out."

The young scientist spoke up again. "You mean the universe is going to turn itself inside out?"

"It is doing so even as we speak. But it will destroy itself long before it ever completes the exercise."

The room was abuzz with conversation, and the scientist nearly had to yell his next question.

"Is there any way to stop it?"

Garrett held up his hand for silence.

"I was coming to that. The fact that the discontinuity is

growing means that Rulisov's machine must still be functioning. Therefore, the lab may still be intact, and the people inside alive. The machine has to be shut down."

"You mean we just turn it off?"

"No. You can't just switch it off. The machine must be modified in order to disengage it from its power source. However, the rift in space/time is so wide that shutting down the machine may not be enough. We have to close the rift itself. To do so, I will have to take one person into the discontinuity and locate its origin. Once there, I will endeavor to install a device in Rulisov's machine to seal the rift."

"What could possibly be powering that thing?"

"The machine is powered by gravitons being drawn from the Earth. I'm sorry, but I don't have time to explain the details."

He paused again, and several hands shot up around the room.

"Please, no more questions. I understand your curiosity, but I have neither the time nor the strength. This is the only possible solution I have been able to come up with, and we will get only one chance to try it. On my table in the lab are plans for the device and a few other items that will need to be constructed before we can proceed. They should be self-explanatory. If you will excuse me now, I am going to get some rest."

Garrett left the shelter before anyone could protest. At first the team members stared at each other blankly. Then all of a sudden as one body they swarmed into the lab, eager to get started on the plans Garrett had drafted in the early hours of the morning.

The first set of plans called for extensive modifications to two environment suits. The handwritten title at the top of the drawing read *Neutron Regulated Graviton Field Generator*.

There was nothing on the component list that the technicians did not recognize, but none of them had ever seen the pieces assembled quite this way. According to the plans, the finished generator would be about the size of a cereal box, mounted on the chest, with tiny cables winding over the entire surface of the suit.

The second set of plans was entitled *Systemic Graviton Inducer*. For such an imposing name, the inducer was a mundane-looking device. Shaped like a small transmission tower with components and adapters in the middle, the inducer stood only ten inches high. Again, the technicians recognized the components but not the configuration.

The third set of plans read simply *Graviton Bomb* and consisted of a simple cannister equipped with a device capable of emitting a graviton burst. The technicians were nodding. They had seen this type of thing before. High-intensity graviton emitters were widely used in particle accelerators. Then one of them noticed the quantity of cannisters ordered.

"Seven thousand two hundred? Who does he think we are?"

The final set of plans was for a simple hopper with a feed mechanism and a gun for deploying the cannisters. The hopper was twelve feet long by six feet high, designed to hold thirty-six hundred cannisters, or half the total amount. The feed mechanism loaded the cannisters one by one into the gun, where they were fired at one second intervals and low velocity.

The leader of the group, Dr. Lionel Merrick, quickly divided the group into teams according to skill, setting them to work on each of the four projects. He handpicked three workers to help him implement the acquisition of the considerable volumes of materials required for each project, in addition to coordination of the industrial manufacturing services that were going to have to be secured.

They were only a few minutes into the operation when the first team hit a snag. Because of the severe conditions and the number of ships recently departed from Earth, there was a shortage of environment suits. Two technicians hurried over to the main shelter to chase one down with the comm chief.

Jerry had spent the morning trying to find something useful to do. He walked into the main shelter just as one of the technicians was trying to talk some commercial pilot out of his environment suit. Jerry calmly walked over and offered to give them the two from his ship. The two technicians looked at him with some disbelief, but followed him out of the shelter.

Jerry led them up the ramp onto the LX44 and opened up the storage compartment. Two shiny new environment suits, neither of which had ever been worn, hung motionless in the compartment. Nearly drooling, the technicians removed the suits, thanked Jerry profusely and scurried back to the lab. Jerry watched them go and smiled, once again at loose ends.

Two hours later, the first three projects were well underway. The fourth was being coordinated through two large industrial manufacturers located in Cincinnati and Detroit, which were working on the cannisters and hoppers.

The hoppers were to be fabricated out of plastic, extremely light and stronger than steel. The tops were fitted with a flexible collar, to allow them to be installed on any of a number of air- or spacecraft.

Through it all, Garrett slept soundly, never moving on his cot in the makeshift visitors' tent. At the end of ten hours, his chronometer beeped and he sat up. The first thing he heard from inside the shelter was the sound of helicopter engines, and he stepped outside to an impressive sight.

Four jet helicopters sat parked in the snowy field, while soldiers in snowsuits unloaded the first crates of cannisters. As he walked out into the staging area, Garrett nearly bumped into Dr. Merrick. The hoppers and feed mechanisms were being airlifted from Detroit, he explained, and the balance of the cannisters were either en route or being packed for shipping. The suits and inducer were nearly ready for testing.

"Thank you for all your hard work, Doctor Merrick. Please let me know when everything is ready and we'll have a final briefing."

Dr. Merrick nodded, and Garrett went to search for Chris. He tried the main shelter first, but found only the communications officer.

"Have you seen Nathan or his son?"

"Not since last night."

He left the main shelter and began searching the smaller ones nearby. Several minutes later, he found Chris and Nathan's tent. They were both asleep. He gently shook Chris to wake him and crouched down by his cot.

"Chris, I need to talk to you," he said in a low voice, glancing over to be sure Nathan was not disturbed.

Chris didn't open his eyes. "What do you want?"

"I want you to go with me into the discontinuity."

His eyes fluttered open, and he winced. "Why me?"

"You know how I think. You're good under pressure. I know your capabilities. Shall I go on?"

"No. That's enough. Assuming we actually go inside that thing, what are we going to do when we get there?"

"Our first priority is to close up the discontinuity."

"I would think it's our *only* objective."

"No. There are some other things to consider. The utility company report says that the power spike that blew that big hole in the street may have been caused by a catastrophic capacitor overload."

"Catastrophic overload usually means explosive, doesn't it?"

"Yes. We have to be ready for the possibility that your brother and everyone in the lab is already dead. If they're not, we may be able to help them. We may not even be able to save ourselves. If we are successful and time resumes its course, we could easily find ourselves incinerated by the explosion."

"Nice thought."

"I just want to be sure you know what you're getting into. Our last objective is to try to keep the backlash from exiting the building and killing those people down on Colfax Avenue when the breaker explodes."

"You don't want much, do you? How are we going to do that?"

"I don't know yet. It depends on how mixed up the time streams are. It may be so jumbled in there, we can't do anything." He straightened up. "We should get moving."

Chris woke Nathan, who took a moment to get his bearings before he could focus. Chris explained Garrett's plan, and though Nathan did not like the idea of putting his son at risk, he knew Garrett would not have asked if it weren't important.

The three men walked out of the shelter and headed straight for the lab. Inside, the team was putting the finishing touches on the suits, and the inducer was already being tested. Off to the right, Jerry stood with his back against the wall, watching indifferently with his arms crossed. Chris walked over to him.

"I didn't think you were serious about staying."

"Garrett asked me to. Besides, my commander's going to want to know the fate of those environment suits."

Garrett turned to Nathan. "Doctor Graham, will you contact the Air Force base and ask them to scramble one IPF fighter and be here in twenty minutes?"

Nathan was too exhausted to care much about anything at the moment. "I'll try."

He walked out the door and over to the main shelter, and called the Air Force base.

Lieutenant Nolan Thomas was sitting in the reading room at the IPF Base near Denver, reading up on the latest in propulsion developments, when suddenly his emergency scramble alarm went off. Thomas reached down to his belt and switched the thing off, wondering what inane mission base command had for him this time.

He jogged the half mile to the hangar; being in excellent shape, he wasn't even winded when he reached the door. The base chaplain walked into the hangar minutes later, as Thomas was suiting up, and began to pray over his fighter, as he did anytime there was an emergency mission.

Thomas was a little uncomfortable with the ritual. "You know that really isn't necessary."

The chaplain smiled kindly and made the sign of the cross on the fuselage. "Oh, but it is, my boy. Someday, you may be glad for it."

Lieutenant Thomas shrugged and rolled his eyes, climbing up into the cockpit.

Back at the camp, inside the lab, Jerry was watching Garrett explain to Chris how the environment suits worked.

"They're just like normal suits, except the outside surface is

117

covered with small cables that are attached to this unit on the chest. This generates a neutron-regulated graviton field."

"Neutron-regulated?"

"Yes. There's a sensor on the front that measures the frequency vibrations of the antigraviton waves. The inverse of that frequency is used to automatically calibrate a neutron condenser inside the chest unit. By passing the gravitons through the condenser, the graviton emissions are released at the inverse frequency, creating a shield."

"You mean, the same way sound waves of equal and opposite amplitude cancel each other out?"

"Something like that. If it works, we should be protected from the effects of the discontinuity. If not, we will most likely be lost in time forever."

Chris ran a hand through his hair, wondering why he couldn't have friends who did normal things, like quietly climbing the corporate ladder. Twenty minutes later, they heard the roar of an engine and stepped outside to a great flurry of snow. The IPF fighter touched down next to Jerry's ship, and the engines shut down. The pilot climbed out and Garrett hurried to meet him.

"Lieutenant Nolan Thomas, reporting for duty."

"Thank you, lieutenant. Come with me, please."

The worker team had already gathered outside the lab to greet the new arrival, and swiftly went to work attaching the hoppers to the undersides of the fighter and the LX44.

Everyone else squeezed into the main shelter for a final briefing. Garrett stood in front of the group again.

"I want to thank you all. Your work has been exemplary. I'm sorry for not going into more detail earlier, but I appreciate your efforts under these circumstances."

A young technician up front was overwhelmed with curiosity. "What happens now?"

"Now, Lieutenant Thomas and Jerry Wysoski will take off and fly in opposite directions along the discontinuity at point two five of light speed, deploying the cannisters into the time distortion."

An older scientist raised his hand. "How can they fly along the discontinuity? If it sticks out from the North American continent, as Earth rotates it must be whipping all around the solar system."

"That was true, at first, but the last satellite transmission we received indicates that our orbit around the sun is stabilizing. It also shows that the same gravimetric flux that warped Earth's orbit has had another interesting result. The discontinuity has become the planet's new axis of rotation."

"You mean Denver is now the North Pole?"

"Yes, but the angle of Earth is skewed, which accounts for the unusual position of the sun. Regardless, the discontinuity should provide a very stable flight path from its point of origin. While they deploy the cannisters, Chris Graham and I will put on the environment suits and enter the discontinuity. I hope to find the center and Rulisov's lab, and use the inducer you constructed to detonate the cannisters, thereby neutralizing the effects of her machine. Now, if there are no further questions, let's get started."

The briefing broke up. Some of the technicians left to make final adjustments on the suits and to verify that installation of the hoppers was going smoothly. Several people clustered around Garrett for last minute discussion. The first in line was the inquisitive technician who had spoken up earlier.

"We outfitted your utility belt with the tools you requested. We wanted to be sure you really meant to take along a three-foot iron rod."

"Yes, I need the rod."

Next in line was Lieutenant Thomas. "You said we're supposed to deploy the cannisters at a speed of point two five of light speed. My top speed is point two, fully loaded."

Garrett pursed his lips for a moment and then scanned the room, finally locating Jerry near the door talking to two engineers. "Jerry! Could you come over here for a minute?"

Jerry joined them and Garrett turned so that it would be a three-way conversation. "Lieutenant Thomas tells me the top speed of his IPF fighter is point two of light speed, fully loaded.

Can you modify his engine so he can maintain a speed of point two five for at least an hour?"

"I can supercharge the engine, no problem, but there are some parts that won't take the pounding for very long. There's a butterfly valve just before the injectors, which will probably fail first. You'll get about forty-five minutes at point two five, and then you go up in a blaze of glory."

Lieutenant Thomas nodded. "I understand."

Garrett, realizing that Thomas was signing up for a potential suicide mission, put a hand on his arm. They nodded to each other, and Jerry walked with the lieutenant out of the shelter.

"If it makes you feel any better, my trip's going to be one way, too."

The lieutenant was surprised by that. "But you can stick point two five easy."

"Yeah, but I'm not going to have a chance to refuel, and I'm already running on vapor."

There were only two places in the solar system where the LX44 could be refueled, Perimeter Command and Osaka, Japan. As soon as he had heard what Garrett had in mind for the LX44, Jerry had contacted Osaka Base Command, only to find that the base was completely shut down by the cold.

Jerry put his arm around the lieutenant's shoulder as they approached their ships. "Do you know the Twenty-third Psalm?"

The lieutenant shook his head.

"My grandma taught it to me when I was six years old. I never forgot it. It's not a bad thing to know in a situation like this."

By the time Jerry had finished making the modifications to Lieutenant Thomas's fighter, everything was ready. A team of technicians helped Garrett and Chris into their suits. With his tool belt hanging around his waist, Garrett looked like a pudgy alien with varicose veins in a grass skirt.

The final check on the suits was complete, and all that remained to be donned were their helmets. Nathan walked up. The suits made a hug impossible, so Nathan shook their hands.

"God bless you both."

Garrett smiled. "Thanks. We'll need it."

Chris said good-bye to his father. "I love you, Dad."

"I love you, too."

Nathan wiped his eyes and moved back so that preparations could continue. Garrett poked Chris in the shoulder.

"Is there a data cartridge over my right hip?"

Chris looked down. "Yes. The label says G–A–one."

"Good."

They walked out of the lab toward the discontinuity, followed by a small group of technicians carrying their helmets. The fighter and the LX44 were already warming up. The ships looked like queen bees, with the hoppers bulging downward like fat bellies. Chris saw Jerry in the cockpit of his craft and waved. Jerry flashed his most cocky, self-assured grin and gave Chris the thumbs up.

They walked on further, through a temporary security fence, and soon were within fifty feet of the time distortion. Daunted by the swirling chaos in front of him, Chris turned to Garrett.

"Are you sure this is necessary?"

Garrett directed his attention to the edges of the discontinuity. "Do you see those black wisps near the edges? I believe those are actual rips in the fabric of space/time. In a few weeks there won't be any way to stop it. We have about two minutes before the discontinuity overruns our position. Do you want to back out?"

"Of course I want to back out. Even a fool would want to back out. But I won't. Besides, I'd be lying if I said I wasn't curious about what's in there."

He paused and then blurted, "I know this is probably not the best time, but I have to know. Why does that thing make a sound like rushing water?"

Garrett thought for a moment. "I'm not sure, but it's possible that ambient sound waves reflected off large surfaces are bent when the surfaces disappear into the discontinuity. Now, a bit more alacrity, if you please."

The small group of technicians quickly sealed the helmets on the suits, attached the suits with a cable so they wouldn't lose each other, and activated a locator unit on Garrett's wrist. The wrist unit measured antigraviton emissions, giving him a kind of compass for locating the center of the discontinuity.

The technicians were increasingly nervous, but they stood their ground, helping Garrett and Chris check their graviton-modulated communicators and activate the graviton field generators on their chests. The suits began to shimmer, and the technicians beat a hasty retreat.

The snow was nearly hip deep, which made the going very hard, so Garrett motioned to stand still and waited for the discontinuity to overtake them. As the swollen monolith approached, the urge to flee was very strong, but they both knew that was not an option.

"Oh, Lord," Chris prayed, "I can't believe we're doing this. Please send your angels to watch over us, and crown our efforts with success."

"Amen," Garrett said under his breath.

They didn't have to wait long. Like a creeping wall of liquid metal, the distortion advanced and engulfed them where they stood.

The scene changed abruptly, and they both experienced a sense of weightlessness. It took Garrett several seconds to understand what he was seeing. By the look of it, they were floating upside-down at an angle, seventy-five feet above a field.

Down below, outside a small farm house a woman was frozen in the act of hanging laundry. The entire scene had a haziness to it, like a television screen with the brightness all the way up. The only thing moving was the swirling, shimmering surface through which they had come, which formed an enormous canopy over the scene below.

"Garrett, what's happening?" Chris spoke nervously into the mouthpiece of his helmet communicator.

There was no response.

"Garrett! Garrett!"

"I'm here, right next to you!" Garrett turned his body awkwardly until he could see the front of Chris's helmet. "Sorry for not answering right away, but this is all new to me. I need a minute to think."

Outside the discontinuity, the camp headquarters was being torn down and moved back again, and the LX44 and IPF Fighter took off. Both ships roared upward in a precipitous power climb and were quickly out of sight. Once they were clear of the atmosphere, Lieutenant Thomas accelerated and peeled away, racing around the globe to the point where the discontinuity exited from the other side.

He rocketed away from Earth, bringing his ship alongside the time distortion until it was nearly skimming the surface. Jerry was already well on his way in the opposite direction. The lieutenant spoke into his communicator in an effort to contact Jerry.

"LX44, do you copy?"

"Roger that. Increase to point two five and commence cannister deployment."

Lieutenant Thomas pushed open the throttle all the way and nearly passed out from the acceleration, in spite of his pressure suit. Several seconds later, when his head cleared, he spoke into his communicator again.

"Steady at point two five. Commencing deployment."

He reached down to a shabby metal box that looked as if it had been hastily thrown together in someone's garage, and threw a switch. The feed mechanism in the hopper switched on, and the gun began spitting cannisters out the back and into the discontinuity.

On the LX44, Jerry doublechecked to make sure everything was working perfectly, then put the ship on autopilot and spoke into his communicator.

"What's your status?"

"A little shaky, but not bad. Engine's running hot."

"Sorry I didn't have time to modify your autopilot."

Lieutenant Thomas smiled mirthlessly. "For a forty-five minute trip, I can fly on manual."

Jerry could hear the edge in the lieutenant's voice. "At this speed, we'll lose voice contact in about five minutes."

The speaker was silent for a moment before the lieutenant replied. "How does that psalm go again?"

"You gotta think like a sheep."

"Right. 'The LORD is my shepherd. . . .'"

Jerry leaned back in his seat, listening to the soothing words his grandmother had taught him. When the lieutenant made a mistake, Jerry corrected him and had him start over. They went on like that for several minutes, before the signal began to get weaker.

"Looks like I'm losing you, Jerry."

"See you on the other side, Nolan."

A moment later, the receiver went dead.


"I think I've got it," Garrett said, fumbling around with one of the tools on his tool belt.

"Are you going to let me in on it?" Chris asked, a bit testily. Hanging around upside-down was beginning to get on his nerves.

"I believe we have crossed over into another time stream."

"Why is that woman down there frozen like that? And why haven't we fallen?"

"This time stream is an artifact of the antigraviton bombardment from Rulisov's machine at the center of the discontinuity. We are shielded from the effects by the field generators we are wearing. While the woman below us must travel along the time stream lengthwise, we are cutting across it, bisecting a single moment. Because of temporal inertia, we cannot act upon—or be acted upon by—this time stream."

"What do we do now?"

"Pray that some of the laws of physics still apply."

Garrett pulled from his belt an odd-looking gun that had a grappling hook protruding from its front. Holding the gun out straight, he pulled the trigger and the hook launched, playing out a thin cable as it went. The projectile flew through the void past the woman and bounced harmlessly off the grass.

After several attempts, the hook bounced in front of the clothesline. Garrett pulled gently on the cable and the hook caught on the line, which was as rigid as if it were made of steel. A light tug on the cable started him and Chris moving slowly toward the woman.

"Why is the clothesline so stiff?" Chris wanted to know.

"You have to remember, we are not part of this time stream. Temporal inertia makes it very difficult to move an object out of time."

Garrett gave another tug on the cable, and the clothesline bent and the hook slipped off. They continued their downward movement, but now they were floating free.

"Whoa! That's not supposed to happen," Garrett said in surprise.

"I thought you said we couldn't move anything?"

"We shouldn't be able to, unless. . . ."

"Unless what?"

"Unless the graviton field from our suits is extended to anything we touch. If that is true, and it appears to be the case, we must be very careful. If you have to touch something, be sure it is something that is normally safe to touch and isn't already in motion."

"You mean, like, don't grab a bullet that is just coming out the barrel of a gun."

"Exactly. I suspect it would carry its velocity out of the time stream. Also, you should avoid touching people at all costs. They would be drawn out of the time stream, and there is no oxygen out here."

Chris was trying to twist himself around so his feet were toward the ground. "Right. No touching people."

They grabbed hands and awkwardly twisted and turned themselves until they were able to land feet first. The grass underfoot didn't give at all, which made it like landing on metal spikes. Though not dangerous, the sensation was unpleasant.

Chris wiggled his toes until the tingling went away. "I thought you said whatever we touched would be drawn out of the time stream."

"It must take a few seconds for the field to take effect."

As if to corroborate his hypothesis, the grass beneath their feet began to bend. Garrett checked the locator on his wrist and looked up at what would have been the sky, under normal circumstances. He pointed up and away from their current position.

"We want to go that way. We'll have to push off together. On a count of three. Ready, one, two, three."

They pushed off and slowly floated upward.

# CHAPTER 8

Lieutenant Thomas was forty minutes into his flight, and nearly all of his major systems were flashing warning lights. With grim determination, he kept the throttle full on, ignoring the indicators on his control panel. Jerry's estimate gave him only five more minutes, but he felt surprisingly calm.

"God, I just wanted to say, I'm sorry for some of the things I've done," he prayed. "I've never been very religious, but I guess you already know that. I don't really mind dying, but please make this work. Don't let me die for nothing."

Forty-five minutes came and went, and all the joints on the ship were screaming with the stress. The cannisters were still flipping out the back like clockwork, and somehow the ship was still together. Lieutenant Thomas whispered a prayer of thanks. At fifty minutes, he started the Twenty-third Psalm.

"'The LORD is my shepherd; I shall not want. He makes me to lie down in green pastures. . . .'"

Behind the cockpit, the lateral stabilizer began to collapse.

"'. . . Though I walk through the valley of the shadow of death, I will fear no evil; for You are with me; Your rod and Your staff, they comfort me. . . .'"

The heat shield around the engine block buckled, and the injector housing started to shake apart.

"'. . . Surely goodness and mercy shall follow me all the days of my life; and I will dwell in the house of the LORD forever.'"

At fifty-three minutes, the butterfly valve came loose from the main injector and lodged in the fuel intake. The intake blew up, igniting the fuel up the line, and the fighter went up in a blaze of glory.

The explosion of the fighter didn't register on Jerry's instruments, but he knew instinctively that Nolan Thomas was gone. He looked out the side window and saluted, paying his last respects.

At sixty-four minutes, the last cannister was shot into the discontinuity. Jerry pushed the emergency release for the hopper and pulled back on the stick, arching up and away from the surface of the time distortion. The hopper continued along his original course.

He checked his gauges, saw he was nearly out of fuel, and considered his options. He could try to make it back to Earth, but the fuel would be gone before he got there, making the ship a very large and lethal weapon. Besides, even if he made it, the planet would be uninhabitable within a week or so.

A dash for Perimeter Command was possible, but because of Earth's warped orbit and the distance he had flown, he would be dead from dehydration long before they picked him up on their sensors. The big problem with either option was that the ship would be out of control and could easily smash into some passenger ship or densely populated community. He could leave the ship adrift, but there were shipping lanes crisscrossing this part of the solar system, so a drifting ship was a real hazard.

Not wishing to be posthumously guilty of manslaughter, Jerry knew he had to get the LX44 out of harm's way. He pointed the ship toward deep space and throttled up. The engines roared, pushing him back in his seat, but he was almost used to the acceleration by now. He tried to throttle back, but the stick wouldn't move. There were a dozen ways to shut the engines down, but what was the point?

He watched the speedometer climb. As he passed .85 of light speed, the same effect recurred: the red haze, the white flames, the elongation of the cockpit. This time, the engines stayed on full.

The flames intensified and engulfed the surface of the hull, then moved inside, moving over the controls and Jerry's flight suit. The ship passed .95, the controls fused, and Jerry let go.

In the next instant, the mass of the ship and everything on it were converted to energy, dissolving into a spectacular, kaleidoscopic explosion of multicolored light across the mute canvas of infinite space.

Garrett and Chris took the better part of an hour to traverse the distance between the farmhouse and the turbid canopy overhead. They passed through the silvery shell and found themselves in a very different place.

The scene appeared to be in the mountains, but they had no idea which mountains. Emerging only a few feet above the ground, they looked to be about fifty feet from the next wall of the time distortion. They worked their way along the rocky terrain using the grappling hook, but this time when they tried to pass through the distortion, they bounced off as if it were made of concrete.

Chris reached out and touched it. "What's wrong?"

"I don't know."

Garrett set his feet against the rocks and began applying steady pressure to the murky wall in front of him. A moment later, he was pleased to find his arms slowly sinking into the wall. His arms disappeared, and then his helmet began passing through.

"Oh, of course. . . ."

His transmission was cut off as the rest of his body passed through the distortion. Chris set his feet the way Garrett had done, and pushed. The technique worked for him as well, and in a few moments, he was through.

As he emerged from the other side, he could see Garrett a few feet away, suspended in the middle of an ocean.

"Garrett, can you hear me?"

"Yes. Are you all right?"

"I'm all right, but I can't move."

"You can move, just not very fast. The sea water is affected by our field generators just like anything else. Use your hands to push yourself along."

Chris pushed as hard as he could and was relieved to find that he moved forward a few inches. After a few minutes he was out of breath from the strain. Garrett could hear him panting.

"Don't work so hard. Just apply steady pressure."

Chris rested for a moment, and then pushed against the hard surface of water behind him, this time moving forward with much less effort.

"Thanks."

"I think I see the next distortion up ahead, so maybe we'll be out of this in a few minutes."

Time outside the discontinuity was passing at a much different rate than it was for Garrett and Chris. In the time it took them to cross the first two time streams, a week had passed in the city of Denver. Most of the members of Garrett's team had given up hope and were simply waiting for the end. Dr. Graham prayed for them both diligently, but had no way of knowing if his intercession was doing any good.

When the deadline came for the European Commonwealth to launch its missiles to destroy the discontinuity, the missiles never made it out of their silos because of the extreme cold. Temperatures were passing one hundred fifty below and showing no signs of leveling off. Most of the populations of the Earth were dead or dying, and the few pockets of civilization still remaining were dwindling by the hour.

In Lakewood, the shelters could no longer be moved as the discontinuity advanced, and the emergency generators were failing. Inside the main shelter, the generator had failed several hours earlier. The communications officer was frozen at his post, and strewn about the floor were the bodies of the city commissioner and the military advisors who had remained vigilant to the last.

Nathan Graham was kneeling alone, praying in his snowbound shelter, when his generator failed. He knew that Amie was probably gone, along with everyone in the hospital, as the facility generator had broken down a few hours before and there was nowhere to evacuate to. Not for anyone. His only thought was that he would be with his family again soon, in the glorious—and warm—presence of God.

The temperature in his shelter dropped rapidly, and he felt very cold at first. But then the sensation of cold left him. He stayed on his knees, closed his eyes, and gradually lost consciousness, forever frozen in a posture of humble supplication. And a lifeless Earth continued its icy march around the sun.

Garrett and Chris worked their way through forty feet of ocean water in a half hour, as they judged the passage of time, and passed through the next time distortion without difficulty.

This time the view was more disorienting. High overhead, there seemed to be part of a city street, but they could only see a slice of it because the next distortion was quite close. With no extra effort, their momentum carried them on through to the next time stream.

Now there was nothing to see except the same silvery, swirling light as they passed from one time stream to the next. Chris called out to Garrett but there was no response. His only connection to anything resembling reality was the tether connecting him to his friend.

After a few minutes, he closed his eyes because he could no longer bear the chaotic view assaulting his eyes. Suddenly, he bumped into something and spun around, as the tether stopped his angular momentum. He opened his eyes and saw a hallway stretching out before him.

"Garrett, can you hear me?" he called in a panic.

Garrett's voice came reassuringly over the communicator. "I hear you. Are you hurt?"

"No, I'm fine. Where are we?"

"If memory serves, I believe we are in the Technology Center. I was here about ten years ago. The lighting was different, but

I'm sure this is it. According to the locator, we want one of the rooms at the end of the hall."

He reached down and felt around on his belt for a minute before producing two sets of handheld suction cups. He handed one pair to Chris. They were closest to the righthand wall, so they began working their way down it toward the end, pulling themselves along the wall with the suction cups. The last door on the right was placarded with a familiar number.

"Laboratory Eighteen. This should be Rulisov's lab."

Orienting themselves vertically, to at least feel as if everything were right side up, they applied steady pressure on the door until it swung slowly inward. They kept their hands on it as long as they could, but it was soon out of reach, and froze again as soon as it left their hands.

The opening was wide enough for them to enter, and as they pulled themselves through, a bizarre tableau met their eyes. The lab was packed with people, all frozen in the act of trying to hurl or shield themselves from something at the front of the room. Chris looked to his left and saw Ryan standing by the door, with his head turned and his eyes tightly shut.

Chris wanted to grab his brother, to protect him, to somehow take him away from all this, but he knew he couldn't touch him. Garrett tapped him on the shoulder.

"There's no way through. We'll have to go over the top."

Using their suction cups, they crawled along the ceiling and dropped down in front of the group. Up front, next to a bank of machinery, Tatiana Rulisov still had her hand on the switch, a look of horrified disbelief on her face. The antigraviton emitter was glowing brightly, while the positron field generator in front of it disgorged wave upon wave of energized antigravitons into the discontinuity.

Beyond the emitter, near the wall, was the capacitor. Caught in the act of exploding, it had cracks all over the casing, but the shape was unmistakable. Garrett moved over to examine the capacitor more closely.

"She didn't even use any blast shielding," he said with disgust.

He looked around the room briefly, then told Chris to follow him, and leapt up to the ceiling and crawled back out into the hallway.

"Where are we going?"

"To look for some shielding."

They searched every lab they could get into, finishing up in a room not far from the time distortion through which they had entered the hallway. In the storage room off this particular lab, stacked in a corner were some thick slabs of polymer material, complete with mounting hardware. Garrett moved over and grabbed a corner of one of the slabs. Chris pushed at the other end, and after almost half a minute, the slab came free and they were able to move.

They had started out of the room when Garrett noticed a computer workstation on a bench by the door. He let go of the polymer slab, leaving Chris unable to move, and walked over to the computer. Without ceremony, he pulled the data cartridge off his belt and inserted it into the computer's cartridge reader.

"What was that?" Chris wanted to know.

"A worm virus. Even if we're successful, I don't know if you and I—as we exist at this moment—will continue. I created a program to search any computer linked to ComNet, which should be almost all of them. If it finds any of my theories which Rulisov used in her experiments, it will overwrite those data with something more harmless."

"Are you sure destroying knowledge like that is the right thing to do?"

"Would you give a loaded gun to a baby?"

"I see your point. What if the virus doesn't work?"

"I've included a note to myself, as a little added insurance."

They carted the blast shield down the hall and into Laboratory 18, carefully maneuvering it over the crowd, and bolted it into place in front of the capacitor. They repeated the process until there were blast shields on three sides and on top, leaving the only opening toward the outside wall.

Chris eyed the shielding speculatively. "Do you think it will hold?"

"I don't know. At least they stand a chance now."

Garrett reached down again and pulled the three-foot iron rod off his belt. Silently he handed it to Chris along with a hammer.

"What's this for?"

"You need to insert the rod into the main power feed, as far down the hall as you can go. You can't miss it. It's the thick, red cable that runs the length of the ceiling in the hallway."

"Why?"

"Since the capacitor was frozen at the same instant it exploded, there's a chance that the power backlash hasn't left the building."

"What if it has left the building? Isn't there some way to verify?"

Garrett scanned the panels at the front of the room, looking for a time counter. The panels were covered with controls, but most of it was stuff he recognized, so he had a pretty good idea where to look.

"Six point two five three seconds. Unfortunately, I have no way of knowing when the backlash happened. Judging from the blast fissures on the capacitor, I would guess only a few milliseconds passed before the explosion. The power surge may or may not have left the building. You might have to try to find a location outside the building."

"How am I supposed to find a location outside?"

Garrett was quiet for a moment. "This is a major facility, there should be an access hole out on the street."

Chris held the rod and hammer at arm's length. "How am I supposed to drive a spike into a cable while it's still in the time stream?"

"You can't. You'll have to position the rod, hold the cable with one hand, and swing the hammer with the other. Once you're through, get clear immediately, because any electrons inside the cable that are within range of your field generator— and there are likely to be a lot—will exit through the rod."

"I don't suppose you're coming with me?"

"I have to stay here and prepare the graviton inducer."

Chris gave his friend a dark look, but he couldn't see his eyes behind the visor. He walked over to the window, and leaned against the glass until the graviton field took effect, then hit the window with his hammer. The glass shattered, but as the shards fell outward, they left the graviton field generated by his suit and froze in midair.

Garrett's voice came over his helmet speaker. "Have you no regard for private property?"

Chris turned away from the window. "If that blast shielding holds, you can kiss this whole wall goodbye."

He cleared away enough of a hole to climb through, and lifted one leg over the sill. Garrett wished him luck, and Chris waved, climbing down to the ground on the other side, before stowing his hammer on his belt. Using the suction cups Garrett had given him, he pulled himself along the side of the building until he reached the front.

"I'm at the front of the building. Can you still hear me?"

Garrett's voice came back loud and clear. "Yes."

"It looks pretty weird out here."

The view was strange indeed, almost as if he were in a fish tank and someone had dropped curtains randomly into the water, obscuring parts of the scene. Bends and folds in the discontinuity were moving like a flag blowing in the breeze, but unlike the discontinuity in the time stream he had started from, the surfaces did not appear to be advancing.

Chris looked across the street to Addenbrooke Park and had to take a moment to rearrange his mindset. There were no emergency shelters, no snow, no burning oil. As he surveyed the scene, he realized it was going to be harder to maneuver outside. Disconnected from Garrett, he had no rope to tie himself off.

Positioning his feet against the wall, holding onto the suction cups to steady himself, Chris looked toward a large tree across the street and pushed off. Floating four feet off the ground, he flew in slow motion across the driveway, the lawn, and then the street. But his aim was off slightly, and he could see he was going to miss the tree by ten feet.

"Oh, no."

Garrett sounded concerned. "What's the matter?"

Chris ignored the question for the moment and threw an arm out in a futile attempt to catch a passing limb, before continuing along his original trajectory. Spinning around until he could see forward, he was relieved to see the front of the Rianna Hotel standing directly in his path.

"I'm all right. I missed the tree I was aiming at, but the hotel is coming up ahead."

He pulled his feet up in front of his body to cushion the impact, and suddenly found himself standing on the front wall of the hotel. Even though he kept his legs bent, his feet started to come away from the wall, and he knew he had to pick another direction and push off before he was left hanging in mid-air.

A large cluster of fir trees on the far side of the street looked like a promising target, and he angled his body upward, pushing off lightly. This time, his trajectory took him upward, and by the time he reached the group of trees, he was forty feet off the ground.

Not wishing to impale himself on the spike-like needles of the tree, he reached for a thick branch sticking out ahead of the rest and grabbed on tight, stopping his momentum.

From up in the tree, he could see much more of the vista below. Chris had a clear view of most of the street all the way to the far side of the park. Studying the street, he finally saw what looked like a manhole cover. The handles on the cover looked like an easy grab, but he was going to have to be right on target.

"I see a manhole. I'm going to try for it."

Sailing through the void once more, it looked at first like he was right on the money. But with a few feet to go he was still too high up and he overshot the manhole by five feet.

Chris tried to absorb the impact with the road without losing his forward momentum. He bounced slowly and headed upward again past the manhole, on a collision course with the far end of a church next to the hotel. This was going to be close. If he missed the church, his trajectory would take him out of this time stream. He might never find his way back.

The top corner of the church came tantalizingly close, but Chris could see he was going to miss it by a few feet. As the building passed out of reach, fear and despair clutched at his heart. He was about to give up when he saw the lightning rod: thrust upward like a spear from the top corner and almost within his grasp.

Chris stretched as far as he could and managed to get the tips of his fingers around the rod. His body swung around the rod, and he carefully brought his other hand over until he had a good grip with both hands, and could stop his rotation. Clinging to the rod for dear life, Chris examined the scene below from his new vantage point.

"Chris? Are you still there?"

Chris paused to take a deep breath. "I'm here. I overshot the manhole, but the view from the top of the church is quite lovely."

Garrett heard the irony in his friend's voice. "Rough trip? Sorry I missed it."

He wanted to tell Garrett just how rough the trip was, but hopefully there would be time for that later. Time for that later. Time later. Chris mused absurdly for a moment about the concepts of *time* and *later* in relation to his current circumstances. If they didn't destroy this thing, there might not be any time at all. Anywhere. Ever.

He had a clear shot at the manhole from here. He was getting better at aiming in the right direction, so maybe this time he could get a hand on the manhole cover. Chris positioned his legs behind him and prepared to push off. Then he saw the car.

Barely fifty feet from the manhole was a ground car. There were no other cars around, but this one would intersect with the manhole at almost the same moment as the backlash exited the cable, assuming Chris was successful in his task. If there was an explosion, the occupants of the car might be killed. Admittedly, this was better than detonating the propane under Colfax Avenue—and killing a dozen people—but Chris was not prepared to sacrifice these people for the sake of the others.

"There's a ground car near the manhole. I'm going to take a look."

Using the wall of the church as a base, Chris launched himself toward the ground car, and this time his aim was true. He grabbed onto a fender and looked the car over from front to back. The rear storage compartment was open, but tied down part way with elastic cords, apparently over a large parcel—a crib, judging from the picture on the side.

Chris peered inside the passenger compartment. The driver was a woman, and an infant was strapped into the passenger seat. With looks of serenity, they were utterly unaware that they were on the brink of catastrophe. Chris was all the more determined to find a way to save them.

"If there is an explosion, this lady and her baby might be killed. Any suggestions?"

Chris received silence in return. He was just about to call out to Garrett again when he answered. "You could try to set the emergency brake."

Remembering the broken window from earlier, Chris placed a hand on the driver's window until the glass was enveloped in the graviton field from his suit. He hit the window with his hammer, and as before, the shards burst inward and then froze in space as they left the graviton field. Chris carefully pulled each piece of glass out of the air, leaving them floating outside the car.

If he could reach the emergency brake, he might be able to set it. But the break was located between the front seats, and there was no way to reach it without touching the driver or the baby if he came from the other side. Breaking out the windshield was an option, but the windshield glass was very strong, and he doubted he could clear a big enough hole to allow him to maneuver. Besides, as he thought about it, all the emergency brake would do is lock the wheels. The car would probably come to a stop right over the manhole.

"No good. They're too close to the manhole."

Garrett paused from his work on the inducer. "Then you need to try and redirect the vehicle."

Chris tried to think what he would do if he were the driver. *Pull off the road.* He looked down the road for oncoming traffic and found none. The driver's hands were on the bottom of the steering wheel. He would still have to get too close to the woman in order to grab the steering wheel. He needed something that would turn the wheel after time began moving again. Then inspiration hit him.

He pulled himself along the side of the car until he was behind it. He grabbed one of the elastic cords and held on until it became pliable, then unhooked both ends. With the cord coiled in one hand he pulled himself back up the length of the car to the broken window.

Looping the elastic through one of the supports inside the far side of the steering wheel, he brought the ends down and around the handle on the inside of the driver's door. He pulled the elastic as tight as he could, made the loop twice more, and then tied the ends off at the door handle. Chris checked his work and decided it would have to do. As for these two innocent bystanders, their lives were in God's hands.

"I secured an elastic cord to the steering wheel. If it catches her by surprise—and it should—the pull should be sufficient to take her off the road."

"You checked for oncoming traffic?"

"Of course."

Chris worked his way round to the front of the car, placed his feet against the grill, and pushed off, floating parallel to the ground two feet up. The manhole cover slowly passed beneath him and he grabbed the handles. The graviton field from his suit encompassed the heavy metal disk, and he found he was able to move it with surprising ease. He set the cover to one side and looked down the hole. It was pitch black.

"I'm at the manhole. Can't see anything."

He started down the hole, hoping his eyes would grow accustomed to the darkness, but a peculiar thing happened. As he moved down the hole, the light that had originally been stopped by the cover, came in contact with his graviton field and began moving down into the darkness, like a faint, swirling mist. He stood still for a moment and then continued his descent. By the time he reached the bottom, some of the light from the hole above was illuminating the tunnel.

"I wish you could see this. The light is following me down the hole, like fairy dust."

Garrett chuckled. "I hadn't considered that possibility. Any photons outside your graviton field will remain stationary. You could actually be standing in direct sunlight and shadow simultaneously. Interesting."

In the odd, half-lit shadows of the passage, Chris was able to make out a group of cables bracketed to the right wall. One of the cables was bigger than the others and bright red. That must be the one. With hammer in one hand and iron rod in the other, he positioned the rod so that the pointed end was touching the surface of the red cable, and grabbed the cable with his left hand. The cable was attached to the wall, so he had no idea when the field generator had done its work. He gave it a minute or so before taking careful aim with the hammer.

Chris delivered the first blow right on target and the rod sank into the cable. Sparks and then an electric arc shot from the rod, and he let go of the cable and lurched away, almost slamming into the ladder. The arc hit him in the leg, tearing a hole in his environment suit, and he heard the terrifying sound of air escaping.

"I'm hit! I'm losing air!"

Garrett's voice was right there. "How big is the hole?"

"I can't see it. Probably a half inch or so, by the sound of it."

"Reach down to the controls at your waist. The far left dial—turn it all the way to the right. That will increase the flow of oxygen."

Chris did as he was instructed. "Got it."

"Now the next dial over, turn it a quarter turn to the right. That will thicken the mixture. If you start to feel giddy or lightheaded, turn it back a bit."

The hissing was still there, but the air in his suit began to feel normal again. "Thanks. By the way, I got the rod into the cable."

"Good work. Now, get back here. I need your help."

Chris scaled the ladder to the street and replaced the manhole cover. With one last look at the ground car, he turned toward the Technology Center, pressed his toes against the handles, and pushed off. His feet slipped, and he floated with maddening slowness toward the side of the Technology Center.

"I'm gonna be a while. I got a slow start."

Chris took a full ten minutes to traverse the distance between the manhole and the side of the building. He had to bank off another copse of trees to get around front and retrieve his suction cups. Tired of bouncing around like a ping pong ball, he gratefully used the suction cups to pull himself back to the lab and Garrett. The hissing inside Chris's suit was unnerving, and Garrett stopped what he was doing long enough to put a patch over the hole in Chris's thigh. The hissing stopped, and Chris readjusted the environment controls on the front of his suit.

Garrett picked up the inducer and stood beside the antigraviton emitter. He motioned for Chris to come around to the far side of the emitter.

"I want you to grab the other side of the inducer. You see the connectors on the bottom? They fit into those slots in the emitter right there. Now, on a count of three, we are going to push the inducer into place, and switch off our field generators."

"Hold it. Switch off our field generators?"

"We can't stay out here forever. And we could never find our way back to where we started, even if we wanted to. Whether you and I as we are now will continue to exist or not, we have to enter this time stream at this point."

Chris nodded. They grabbed the inducer with both hands and inserted it into the antigraviton emitter, switching off their field generators as soon as it was in place. There was a graviton burst from the inducer which traveled the length of the discontinuity, detonating the cannisters dropped by Lieutenant Thomas and Jerry Wysoski. The cannisters released their own graviton bursts and the discontinuity imploded, closing in on itself in an instant.

The scene in the lab snapped into focus for Garrett and Chris for an instant, and the capacitor exploded. A colossal hole blew out in the wall, sending fire and debris spewing a hundred feet across the lawn outside. Simultaneously the force of the explosion sent the blast shield hurtling into Chris. Garrett was slammed through the front wall a moment later, when the shield smashed through the banks of machinery at the front of the room. The force of the blast knocked the audience to the floor. As the debris settled, the echo of the concussion from the blast came back from the trees across the lawn.

Down the street from the Technology Center, the driver of a ground car suddenly lost control of her vehicle and careened across the oncoming lane. The car jumped the curb and plowed onto the lawn of the Rianna Hotel. At the same moment, a tremendous bolt of electricity burned up the iron rod sticking out of the red cable below the street and exited into the tunnel, blasting a twenty-foot hole in the road and sending chunks of pavement in all directions.

Dazed and frightened, the woman in the car checked her baby, who was screaming vociferously, but otherwise unharmed. She noticed her driver's side window was gone and then looked down at her steering wheel. Somehow, inexplicably, an elastic cord had been tied around the steering wheel.

Downtown in the control center for the power company, alarms went off everywhere and on-duty personnel scrambled for their stations. The chief engineer for the shift called out status from the monitoring console.

"Looks like we've had an explosion at the Technology Center. Backlash meltdown on the main power feed. Massive electromagnetic transient near breaker zero three eight."

He pulled up a grid map of the city, with the location of the explosion lit up in red. After a brief assessment, he mumbled to himself, "It may have exited at the Technology Center." He thumbed the communicator.

"Emergency Services, Code Red to J-four-two! Code Red to J-four-two!"

\*    \*    \*

At the edge of the solar system, inside Perimeter Command Station, last outpost for the Interplanetary Police Force—or IPF as they were called—head mechanic Jerry Wysoski was up to his elbows inside the engine of one of the IPF Fighters it was his pleasure to work on every day.

He glanced over at the LX44, an experimental craft built for high speed, and one he had been wanting to take out for some time. He eyed the sleek ship, and suddenly, for no reason at all, the desire to fly it left him. While he was never one to pass up a good thrill, he wasn't stupid.

Jerry shook his head and turned his attention back to the business at hand. At the moment, he wished he were in the pilot's seat. For two hours he had been trying to chase down a pesky electrical problem. He had his probe isolated on the offending connection when the station alarm went off. The noise startled him so badly that he spun sideways, whacking his head on the engine compartment.

With one hand holding his head, he ran out of the launch bay into the control room down the hall. Three officers were manning the various consoles which filled the room, and at the moment each one was very preoccupied by the indicators on his equipment. Several more officers rushed behind Jerry.

"What's going on?" Jerry asked.

A corporal at the sensor terminal, with thin-rimmed glasses and a nickname of *Peels* was trying to make sense of the data on his screen. "We had an anomaly off the port bow for just an instant, but now it's gone."

Jerry thought nothing of the nautical reference, as the console operators, or con ops, were prone to that sort of talk. "Equipment malfunction?"

"Negative. It just disappeared."

Millie Graham was awakened from a sound sleep by a terrible nightmare. She sat bolt upright and took several deep breaths to try and calm herself. She reached beside her, seeking the

143

comfort of her husband, but found nothing. Nathan was gone.

"Nathan!" There was no answer. "Nathan!"

Her husband came in the door, a blanket in one hand.

"Shhh! What's wrong?"

"I dreamed I was run over by a truck, and when I woke up and you weren't there, I got scared."

Nathan sat down beside his wife and gave her a hug. "I'm sorry, sweetie. If I'd known you were going to have a nightmare, I would have waited."

"Where were you?"

Nathan held up a light blue, wool blanket. "I woke up cold. I went to get a blanket."

"A blanket? It's at least eighty degrees in here."

"I was just noticing that."

Amie walked into their room looking very sleepy.

"What's up?"

"Nothing. Your mom had a bad dream, that's all. Go back to bed."

Amie yawned and smiled as if she were already halfway there.

"If you insist."

She walked back to her room and fell into bed, dropping quickly back to sleep.

This particular day at sea was calm, and warm—at least for this time of year in the Gulf of Alaska—and nothing in the weather reports suggested tomorrow would be any different. Not that the weather was much of a concern for a ship the size of the supertanker *Cyprus*. Over a half mile long, weighing millions of tons fully loaded, the gargantuan oil carrier could pretty much ignore anything the sea wanted to throw at her.

Up in the captain's cabin, Jonas Christos sat at his desk, studying a nautical map. This was not the kind of sailing that made him happy to be a captain. Bad weather, rough seas, even a near collision would have been preferable to the monotonous smooth ride the crew had been enjoying for the last two days.

Christos could only assume the crew was still on board. He

hadn't seen anyone since the ship left port. With a crew of eight, making a run they had made a hundred times before in a ship with most of its functions mechanized, there wasn't much need to disturb the captain.

It was with some surprise, therefore, that Captain Christos received an urgent call from his first mate.

"Captain, there's something off the starboard bow!"

Christos walked out of his cabin onto the deck. Off the starboard bow for as far as the eye could see was . . . nothing. The captain stared for a moment at the vast, unchanging, emptiness of the ocean, then walked angrily back into his cabin and called his first mate.

"Mr. Leutchen, I know you're as bored as the rest of us, but I don't much care for being drug 'round on some wild goose chase!"

Lieutenant Nolan Thomas was sitting in the reading room at the IPF Base near Denver, reading up on the latest in propulsion developments, when suddenly his mouth started moving. The words came out effortlessly:

"The LORD is my shepherd; I shall not want. . . ."

He closed his mouth in shock, wondering why those words—which he had never heard before—had popped unbidden out of his mouth. He mulled the experience over for a while, and being the inquisitive sort, decided to pursue it with an expert.

He walked over to the chaplain's office on the other side of the base and knocked on the door. A moment later, the chaplain opened the door. He was a kind man in his early forties.

"What can I do for you, son?"

"Lieutenant Nolan Thomas, sir. This is going to sound crazy, but about twenty minutes ago I was sitting in the reading room, and these words just came out of my mouth, I mean, zing! I'm minding my own business and suddenly my mouth is talking, and I'm not doing it."

The chaplain looked the lieutenant over, wondering if he had been drinking. "What were the words?"

"'The LORD is my shepherd, I shall not want.' Have you heard that before?"

The chaplain's face broke into a broad smile. "Yes, I have. It's the first line from the Twenty-third Psalm in the Bible."

"The Bible? I've never touched it. I've never even been to church. How could those words come out of my mouth?"

"I have an idea, but it might take a little while to explain."

"I have all afternoon."

The chaplain led the lieutenant into his office and closed the door behind them.

In the dorm cafeteria at the Space Sciences Academy on Io, Chris Graham and Garrett Alger were having dinner together, in another attempt by Chris to help his workaholic friend spend time away from his lab. They were halfway through when without warning, their bodies dematerialized, vanishing without a trace. Their clothes fell in a heap where they had been sitting, and several diners nearby screamed.

Witnesses to the terrifying event tried to explain what they had seen, but the school officials suspected a prank and wouldn't believe them. When Manny Hascome heard about the incident, he took Leigh Quintana to the president's office and pleaded with him to mount a search. So persistent were they that the president ordered a full search of the academy, if for no other reason than to get them out of his office.

When the search turned up nothing, the school officials looked into the situation in earnest. Manny had some friends from the biology department do a sweep of the cafeteria, but they found nothing out of the ordinary. Leigh racked her brain to think of all the places Garrett and Chris might be, but a careful search of every building by the security officers only confirmed that the two were not on Io.

Back in Laboratory 18 of the New Denver Technology Center, emergency medical technicians were pouring into the lab to tend to the wounded. Near the hole where one wall had been, two

146

or three people were beyond help. One more died on the way to the hospital.

Chris Graham came to in a pile of rubble, wearing what had once been an environment suit. It was now shredded beyond repair. He sat up and found, to his surprise, that he was completely unhurt. There was not even a bruise.

"Where am I? I was eating dinner. . . ."

His voice trailed off as he noticed his brother lying by the door. He clambered out of the pile of rubble and hurried over to Ryan's side. Other than a scratch on the side of his face, Ryan looked to be in good condition.

"Ryan! Ryan, can you hear me?"

Ryan winced, and his eyelids fluttered open. It took a minute for his eyes to focus, but he recognized Chris right away.

"Hey, big brother. What are you doing here?"

"I don't know. Where are we?"

"The New Denver Technology Center."

Garrett Alger climbed through the hole in the front wall, stumbled over the wreckage, and bashed his leg against a chunk of metal. He winced and looked around the room, dazed. Then he caught sight of Chris and limped over. He, too, was wearing a shredded environment suit.

"Chris? What are we doing here? Weren't we just in the cafeteria?"

"Yeah. Ryan tells me we're at the New Denver Technology Center."

"That's not possible!"

Garrett's mouth hung open and he looked around the room. A team of technicians was carrying the broken form of Tatiana Rulisov out on a stretcher through the big hole in the far wall. Mione Arryoto still lay unconscious on the floor nearby. Ryan sighed, hoping they would be all right.

"Well, so much for my interview."

Chris sat down on a pile of rubble, perturbed, and Garrett joined him. Ryan wandered over to examine the wreckage at the front of the room.

"Help me out here, Garrett," said Chris.

"Mmm."

"We were sitting at a table in the cafeteria."

"Mmm."

"I remember blacking out, but I don't remember falling over."

"Mmm."

"Then we were here. On Earth. In Denver. In a ruined laboratory. Out cold on a pile of rubble."

"Mmm. Whose lab was this, do you suppose?"

"Ryan! Whose lab was this?"

"Tatiana Rulisov," said Ryan sadly.

"*Tatiana Rulisov?*" they echoed in unison.

Chris looked at Garrett suspiciously. "Your theories have anything to do with teleportation?"

"Not that I'm aware of. But it's a reasonable bet whatever she was demonstrating is somehow responsible for our being here."

Their conversation was cut short as one of the emergency medical teams reached them. The medics started checking them over.

"Judging from the condition of your suits, you guys must have been pretty close to that thing when it blew," said the first medic.

The other was perplexed. "There's not a mark on you. Do you know how much force it takes to do this to an environment suit?"

"You two should be dead. We'd better take you in for a full examination."

The trip to the hospital in an ambulance was made in silence. After a thorough going-over by the doctors, Chris and Garrett were free to go. Ryan charged some clothes for them from an all-night store nearby using his dad's ID card, and then they returned to Ryan's hotel room to call home.

After several rings, a sleepy voice answered. "Nathan Graham."

"Dad, it's Chris."

Nathan was wide awake in an instant. For his son to call at all was unusual, and the late hour meant almost certainly that some catastrophe had occurred. "Chris? What's wrong? Where are you calling from? It sounds like you're right next door."

"Slow down, Dad. This is going to be hard enough to explain. I'm calling you from Denver. About an hour ago, Garrett Alger and I . . . well . . . just popped into a lab at the Technology Center. We don't know why or how, but we suspect it had something to do with Tatiana Rulisov's experiment."

"Is Ryan with you?"

"Yes, and we're all fine. There was an explosion in the lab. Some of the people didn't make it, but at least she used blast shielding."

"Let me get this straight. An hour ago, you were on Io, and then you just . . . appeared in Rulisov's lab?"

"Sounds crazy, I know. But that's what happened. Even Garrett doesn't know what could cause such a thing. Anyway, we're all here together and we're all right. I thought we would come home for a few days and try to sort this out."

"There was an explosion?"

"Yeah. Garrett and I were wearing a couple of shredded environment suits when we woke up."

"Woke up? You were unconscious? What about Ryan?"

"Listen, Dad, it's all very strange. We can talk about it when we get there. Right now, I just want to get out of here."

"Okay. We'll look for you some time tomorrow."

"Oh, one other thing. Would you please call someone at the Academy? Manny and Leigh are probably worried sick."

"I will."

Nathan terminated the connection and keyed in the long sequence of numbers to put him in touch with the comm operator at the Space Sciences Academy on Io.

"Space Sciences Academy."

"This is Doctor Nathan Graham. May I speak with Manny Hascome, please."

"One moment . . . I'm sorry, there's no answer."

"This is an emergency. Please have him paged."

Four minutes later, Manny came on the line. "This is Manny Hascome."

"Manny, it's Nathan Graham."

"Oh, Doctor Graham, I'm so glad you called! You'll never believe what happened."

Nathan took a deep breath. "Let me guess. Chris and Garrett disappeared and are nowhere to be found."

"How did you know?"

"Chris just called me from Denver. He and Garrett are both there."

"That's impossible."

"I know. Nevertheless, they are both in Denver. Please pass the word along. Chris will be back at our house some time tomorrow afternoon. Maybe he can explain."

"Thanks for calling."

Nathan set the communicator down and put his head back down on his pillow. A muffled, sleepy voice came from the pillow on the other side of the bed.

"What was that all about?" Millie asked.

Nathan started to open his mouth but thought better of it.

"We'll talk about it in the morning."

# Epilogue

In the weeks that followed, Garrett's ongoing efforts to unravel the mystery proved fruitless. Despite numerous attempts to decipher the events at the Technology Center that night, no one was able to explain the sudden appearance of two students from the Space Sciences Academy on Io, at an experiment in Denver, on the planet Earth. The explosion and resulting investigation made headlines for a few days; but when new developments stopped coming, the event was largely forgotten.

With the unofficial investigation at a stalemate, after three weeks in Arlington, Garrett and Chris booked passage back to Io. On the eve of their departure, Ryan suddenly realized he had a gold mine for a professional interview with Garrett, and cornered him in the Graham living room with pencil and paper.

"Okay, what's your full name?"

"Garrett Horatio Alger."

"You're kidding. *Horatio?*"

"My mother told me my father used to read inspirational short stories when he was a child. The hero of the stories was named Horatio Alger."

"How old are you?"

"Twenty-nine and holding."

"Education?"

"High school equivalency, B.S. in Physics, minor in Religion, Masters in Philosophy, Ph.D.'s in Physics, Chemistry, Biology, Artificial Intelligence, Psychology, and Mathematics. I'm currently working on a doctorate in Computer Science."

"Significant papers?"

"Hundreds. Look it up on EDNET."

"I tried to read an article on one particular subject, but it was way over my head. In your own words, what is Subtemporal Irrelativity?"

"You know that everything is made up of atoms, and that atoms are made up of smaller particles—quarks, muons, gluons, mesons, and so forth—and that sub-atomic particles are made up of even smaller particles—chils, nuls, spirs, runts. The list goes on. I came up with several series of equations, one of which proves that relativity breaks down when you reach this lowest known level of particle. Opposites no longer attract. For every action, there is no equal and opposite reaction. Time is no longer linear, or affected by gravity."

"What do you mean, *Time is no longer linear?*"

"I don't know. Some of the equations seem to suggest that one or more of these particles exist in all moments at once. They do not experience duration."

"Cool. So, what was Tatiana Rulisov trying to accomplish, and where did she mess up?"

"Miss Rulisov believed she could push an object forward in time using antigraviton bombardment. Her mistake was mathematical, and probably beyond the reach of your teacher."

"Try me."

"In lay terms, she fiddled around with the gravitational constant, and got burned."

Ryan was scribbling frantically, ". . . *constant, and got burned.* Great quote. So, tell me. Have you ever wanted to be married?"

"What does that have to do with time, space, and dimension?"

"Everything, if you don't want to go through life as a target for everyone's jokes."

Garrett understood all too well. His eyes softened as he realized Ryan was, in some ways, a kindred spirit.

"The answer to your question is, yes. In fact, I am even now pursuing a relationship with an attractive woman, who also

152

happens to be one of the finest biochemists I know. Once you get out of high school, people begin to like you *because* you're smart. Don't ever let some half-wit keep you from doing what you enjoy, just because he doesn't have half the ability God gave a head of lettuce."

"But what if people make fun of you?"

"Be the best you can be, and ignore them. You're not in competition with anyone to be yourself. You are uniquely qualified to be you. No one can do it better. Not even me. Besides, if you won't be you, and I won't be me, who's going to be us?"

Ryan laughed, and kept taking notes. Some of the notes wouldn't go into his paper, but he knew he would carry them in his heart for the rest of his life.

The day Chris and Garrett left for Io, Tatiana Rulisov was charged with negligent homicide in the deaths of ten people at the demonstration.

In the months to come, she would be acquitted, but not before learning some valuable lessons in humility. The judge ordered her to make restitution to the families of the people who were killed, and she was forced to go back to school for her teaching certificate, in order to earn a livelihood. Through it all, she slowly learned that there are more important things in life than research.

Upon Garrett's arrival at the academy on Io, Data Security Administration informed him that a computer virus had been discovered on ComNet. The program was very specialized, designed to seek out and destroy certain details of his research.

Garrett was mystified as to who would want to destroy his research until he read the last letter in his mailbox. The letter was addressed to him, from himself, and described in detail the events from the creation of the discontinuity, to their attempt to destroy it, including the worm virus. He thought the letter a gag until he saw how it was signed: *The Big White G of Garibaldi*.

He memorized the facts in the message, then destroyed it and went looking for Chris. A knock on his dorm room door produced no answer, so Garrett went looking for Leigh's room.

No answer. He checked the library, the recreational center, and was about to check the music hall, when he realized he had overlooked the most likely place on campus.

Chris sat with Manny and Leigh in the lounge at the Student Union Building, nursing an enormous hot fudge sundae. Garrett walked over quietly and waited to be noticed. He hated to interrupt the festivities. Leigh and Manny were so glad to have him back. Manny was the first to see Garrett.

"Hey! It's the Amazing Alger. Great trick, Garrett, but the disappearing act needs work."

Chris snorted into his ice cream. "You should see him saw a lady in two."

Leigh was not so lighthearted. "You won't be doing anything like that again, I take it?"

Garrett smiled. "No. Not likely. At least, I hope not."

Chris scooted over to make room. "Have a seat."

"Actually, I came by to invite you back to my lab. I have some answers to those puzzles we were working on."

Chris looked curiously at Garrett. "Puzzles? Wh . . . Oh! *Those* puzzles." He stood up, the hot fudge sundae forgotten. "Listen guys, this has been great. Thanks so much, but I gotta run. Let's have dinner together, okay?"

Without waiting for an answer, Chris hurried out of the SUB with Garrett. Leigh watched him go and shook her head. "That must be some puzzle to make him abandon a hot fudge sundae."

Manny moved the bowl in front of his place matter-of-factly and started eating. "His loss."

In Garrett's lab in Folsom Hall, Garrett was trying to explain the gist of the strange letter. The story was hard to grasp.

"What do you mean, Rulisov almost destroyed the universe?" Chris was incredulous.

"Her experiment created a split—or discontinuity—in the time stream. The fabric of space/time began to unravel. You and I traveled into the discontinuity and shut her machine down. That's why we materialized in her lab."

"How long did we exist in this other time stream?"

"Best estimate—about three weeks."

"But why don't we have any memory of it?"

"Because it never happened. When the time stream sealed itself, the other time streams ceased to exist. But the patch wasn't perfect. Remember the environment suits we were wearing? We were probably killed when we entered this time stream and the capacitor exploded. Reality—the fundamental laws of existence—could not tolerate two sets of us. Our bodies in Rulisov's lab were replaced by our bodies from the academy."

"I'm glad it wasn't the other way around."

Garrett adjusted his glasses. "Quite."

Chris sat down, trying to take it all in. "We should tell my family."

"There's more. Apparently someone named Jerry Wysoski was. . . ."

"Jerry Wysoski?"

"You know this person?"

"He's a friend. Do you have any details?"

"Not much. Apparently he and a Lieutenant Thomas were instrumental in closing the space/time rift. They must be remarkable people for me to make mention of them in a note like that."

"Now I really do have to tell my family. They all know Jerry."

Garrett looked very serious. "Make sure it doesn't go any further, unless you want all of our lives dissected by the entire scientific community."

Chris knew how ruthless scientists could be when they smelled a new theory.

"Right. But tell me, honestly, who would believe it?"

One month following the accident at the New Denver Technology Center, an emergency team from the gas company pinpointed a propane leak in a tunnel under Colfax Avenue in Lakewood, Colorado. During the repair process, a pipe wrench was discovered wedged between the breaker on the main power feed and the bottom of the breaker box. The name on the wrench was Lenny Consiglio, so they sent it to the power company safety division with a note saying where it had been found.

Lenny's supervisor was not pleased.

During a routine maintenance check at Perimeter Command, two environment suits turned up missing from the LX44. The commander was notified immediately, and the entire company gathered for an emergency meeting.

"All right, you bulkheads! I want to know who stole the environment suits from the LX44!"

A pilot raised his hand. "You really steamed up over a couple of environment suits?"

"No, Scrap Head. It's not the environment suits. *It's everything on this station!* Sure it's just a couple of environment suits this time, but next time it'll be spare parts, or your flight suit, or some of Jerry's tools. I want to know who did this, so I can kick him all the way back to Earth!"

When a station-wide search produced nothing, everyone was confined to quarters until further notice. After a few hours, the commander figured he had made his point, and the suits were listed as missing, presumed lost.

Meanwhile, Jerry Wysoski had been having a recurring dream. He was sitting in the cockpit of a spaceship, one he didn't recognize from the inside. He was looking out the front window, and there was snow on the ground. As he finished the preflight sequence, Chris Graham walked past the front of the ship, and Jerry gave him the thumbs up. Then he woke up.

The dream was always the same. It wasn't a nightmare, but each time he woke up feeling uneasy. The evening after the suits were listed as missing, Jerry had the dream again. He sat up in his bunk, and this time his upper lip was beaded with cold sweat. There was no chance of going back to sleep, so he pulled on his pants and went for a walk.

The station had a different feel about it when everyone was asleep: calm and peaceful, without a hint of urgency. Jerry walked the halls, mulling the dream over and over and found himself taking the usual path from his room to the launch bay.

The rows of small ships all looked the same, except for one. The LX44 sat in the shadows, and somehow, tonight it looked different. Jerry crossed over to the experimental craft, the metal floor of the bay cold underneath his bare feet, and operated the controls to deploy the ramp.

He had never been inside the ship before, and yet something about the ramp coming down was hauntingly familiar. Jerry walked up the ramp and through the short passage to the cockpit. He froze. This was it, the cockpit from his dream, only there was no snow out the front window.

Jerry prided himself on having nerves of steel, but this was too strange. The skin on the back of his neck prickled, and he turned and ran down the ramp into the launch bay. Something about that ship wasn't right, and he needed answers.

One of the few posts that was manned twenty-four hours a day was communications operations, and the comm op did not seem the least bit surprised to see Jerry walking barefoot in the wee hours of the morning.

"Morning, sir. What can I do for you?"

"I need to talk to someone at the Space Sciences Academy on Io."

"You got it."

The comm op took a thick book off his shelf and paged through until he found the correct comm code. He keyed in a long string of numbers, and in moments a voice came over the speaker.

"Space Sciences Academy."

"This is Jerry Wysoski at Perimeter Command. I need to talk to Chris Graham."

"It is quite late here. Is this an emergency?"

"Yes, it is."

After a short wait, Chris's voice came over the line. "Jerry?"

"Hey, preppie. Sorry to interrupt your beauty sleep, but I need to talk to you."

"Go ahead."

"Just a sec." Jerry motioned for the comm op to leave the room.

The man nodded and headed for the door. "I'll be in the officers' lounge."

Jerry waited until he was alone, before continuing. "I've been having this recurring dream. I'm in the cockpit of a spaceship, and out the front window there's snow on the ground. While I'm doing the preflight check, you go walking by and I give you the thumbs up."

"That's it?"

"That's it. But tonight I had the dream again and couldn't get back to sleep. So I take a walk and end up in the launch bay. We have this experimental craft called the LX44. She's supposed to be fast. Anyway, I walk inside, and the cockpit is just like the one in my dream, but I've never been inside the ship before."

Something Jerry said snagged Chris's memory. "This ship has a modified Bussard/Osaka ramjet, right?"

Jerry was shocked. "How did you know that?"

"I don't know. Maybe you told me. Listen, I have something to tell you. It's going to be hard to believe, and you can't ever tell another living soul."

"I'm listening."

Chris proceeded to recount Rulisov's experiment, the split in the time stream, and the imperfect patch effected by Garrett, with the help of Chris, Jerry, and Lieutenant Thomas. The story took almost an hour to explain, and Jerry was drowsy by the end. The lateness of the hour dulled his usual skepticism, and helped him to accept the strange tale.

"So in this other time stream, I may have been on Earth with you? And there might have been snow on the ground?"

"It's very possible."

"Well, that's a relief. At least I'm not going crazy. I've probably taken enough of your time. We gotta get that budding intellect of yours back to bed. Thanks, Chris. Your secret is safe with me."

"Glad to do it. If you're ever out Jupiter way, stop by and see me."

"You can count on it."

Jerry terminated the connection, stuck his head in the officers' lounge to tell the comm op he was through, and sauntered back to his quarters. Maybe he could secure a detail over to Jupiter some time in the next few weeks. Some of the guys at Perimeter Command might enjoy a chance to harass some academy brats.

Jerry said a silent thank you to the God of the universe, as he did every night, and asked Him to bless and keep Chris Graham. Then he rolled over and fell into a deep, dreamless sleep.

An excerpt from *The Mines of Venus*, book four in the Perimeter One Adventures series:

By the time Brice dropped them off at their room, it was late afternoon, though the filtered sunlight had not changed in intensity. It would be just as bright as it was when they arrived for many days to come.

Brice reminded Nathan of their meeting at nine o'clock the following morning and bid everyone good night. Nathan closed the door to their suite, listening carefully for receding footfalls in the hall, and then turned and called a family conference.

"I'd like to get everyone's impressions of what we've seen so far," he said casually, dropping into one of the large easy chairs.

Chris sat down on the sofa, poised for action. "Well, for starters, Brice was lying."

Nathan smiled approvingly. "You noticed it, too?"

Chris nodded. "Those buildings weren't damaged by any seismic activity. They were poorly constructed."

"I got a good, close look at one of the structures. The pieces look as old as the dome itself."

"Did you notice the people? They looked like actors on a stage," Millie added from a corner chair.

Not wanting to be left out, Amie jumped in. "I don't think any of them were for real."

Nathan was interested. "Why do you say that?"

"The phony smiles, for one thing. When one of the ladies walked by, I noticed a split in her dress, and she had another dress on underneath."

Nathan paused thoughtfully. "The question that remains to be answered, then, is *Why?*"

Unfortunately, no one had an answer to that. One by one, Amie, Chris, and Ryan found something to distract them in the suite. Millie prepared dinner in the well-stocked kitchenette, and Nathan turned to his notes for the meeting in the morning. One thing was certain—he had some serious questions for Brice Maddock.